High Praise for ~~Simon Wood~~

"He writes like a dark demented angel."
—Ken Bruen, author of *Priest*

"Simon Wood packs his books with suspense, surprises & superb storytellying."
—Ed Gorman, author of *Sleeping Dogs*

"Simon Wood offers a literary roller coaster ride that thrills and terrifies on every page."
—Sean Chercover, author of *Trigger City*

"Simon Wood is the 'Gary Oldman' of mystery fiction."
—Tony Broadbent, author of *The Smoke*

"When Simon Wood is at the wheel, hang on for a page turner."
—Chris Grabenstein, author of *Hell Hole*

"A supremely gifted writer."
— Jason Pinter, author of *The Mark*

THE
FALL GUY

Simon Wood

WWW.COMETPRESS.US

A Comet Press Book

First Comet Press Trade Paperback Edition
November 2011

The Fall Guy first appeared in *Working Stiffs*, published by
Blue Cubicle Press, 2006.

ISBN 13: 978-1-936964-45-1

Visit Comet Press on the web at: www.cometpress.us

About The Author

Simon Wood is an ex-racecar driver, a licensed pilot and an occasional private investigator. Originally from the UK, he now calls California home. Simon has had over 150 stories and articles published. His short fiction has appeared in a variety of magazines and anthologies, and has garnered him an Anthony Award and a CWA Dagger Award nomination, as well as several readers' choice awards. He's a frequent contributor to Writer's Digest. He's the author of *Working Stiffs, Accidents Waiting To Happen, Paying The Piper, We All Fall Down, Terminated* and *Asking For Trouble*. As Simon Janus, he's the author of *The Scrubs* and *Road Rash*. Curious people can learn more at www.simonwood.net

PART ONE
FENDER BENDER

Todd raced back to his car, cursing the ATM all the way. Why was there always a line? His job packing boxes for a firm in Oakland wasn't much, but he didn't want to lose it by being late again. They'd find a way of firing him sooner or later anyway. Although a monkey could do his job, they'd be better off hiring one. His workmanship, even by his own admission, sucked. But this was his plight. When it came to him and jobs, they never lasted. Okay, he lacked the interest, but irrespective, he also lacked the skill set for any job he undertook.

He hopped back into his car, glad not to see a parking ticket glued to the windshield, and crunched it into reverse. The Honda Accord was way overdue for an overhaul, although an overhaul wouldn't do much for its ancient transmission. It was toast. Half the time, he didn't know what gear he was selecting. The Accord stuttered in the parking spot.

"Get in there, damn it."

Gears snarled as Todd struggled to find a forward gear. He jumped off the clutch and the car leapt backwards, slamming into a Porsche Boxster's headlight.

"Shit," he muttered.

His antics had drawn quite a crowd and they'd all witnessed his screw-up. *Nowhere to run*, he thought. He found first gear without effort this time and eased the Accord forward to assess the extent of the damage.

Everyone had an opinion and had no problem telling him where he'd gone wrong and how much it was going to cost him. He crouched in front of the Porsche and picked at the broken headlight and buckled bumper. There was a couple hundred dollars of damage to the average car, but on the German exotic, he was looking at thousands. His car, the piece of shit that it was, didn't exhibit any signs of damage—just like Todd, who didn't exhibit any signs of insurance.

"Does anyone know who the owner is?" Todd asked.

No one did.

"You'll have to wait," someone suggested.

"I can't. I'm late for work."

"I don't think you have much choice," someone else said.

"I can't. I've been late twice this week already." Todd delved inside his car for a scrap of paper and a pen. "I'll leave a note."

He wrote: *People think I'm leaving you my contact and insurance details. I'm not. Sorry.*

Todd folded up his note, wrote sorry on the outside and stuck it under the windshield wiper. He shrugged, hopped inside the Accord and raced off.

He felt guilty for shafting the Porsche driver, but at the same time, he was buzzing with the thrill of his lawlessness and his speedometer showed it. He was accelerating past forty-five on Telegraph. He took a deep breath and eased off the gas.

In the scheme of things, what he'd done wasn't so bad. It was an accident and it was more likely the Porsche driver's insurance could afford the repairs than he could. *Anyway, with a car like that,* he thought, *you're asking for trouble.* Todd pulled into his employer's parking lot safe in the knowledge that the matter was over.

* * *

Todd liked to take Sunday mornings easy. He lounged in bed until ten then took a walk to the newsstand to pick up the Sunday paper. He wandered back through the apartment complex, pulling out the color supplement and flicking through the magazine, ignoring the front-page splash about some big drug bust. He took a different route back to his apartment and passed close to his assigned parking space. He slowed as he got close to his car. At first, he'd thought his windows had steamed up overnight, but the weather conditions hadn't been right for that. As he closed in, he realized he'd been way off. Every one of the Accord's windows had been smashed and all four tires had been slashed. He ran a hand over the scarred paintwork. A hook end of a crowbar protruded from the front windshield, and a note was sticking out from under a wiper. He pulled it out and read it. "Guess who?" it said.

Todd didn't need to guess. He knew who had done the damage. It was the Porsche owner. Todd hadn't forgotten about the fender bender, but it had been days since it happened and he thought it was over, a stunt that would dissolve in his memory over time. Well, he just found out his stunt was insoluble.

He'd screwed up this time. Someone must have taken down his license plate before he'd driven away. He was going to pay big for this one. He tugged out the crowbar and tossed it on the backseat through a glassless side window.

Returning to his apartment, a thought dogged him. Someone may have reported him to the police or Porsche driver, but how did the Porsche driver know where he lived? He opened the door to his apartment.

"Mr. Todd Collins, I presume," the small man said, getting up from Todd's couch.

Two linebacker types, one black, the other Hispanic, flanked the small man. The small man seemed genial, but the linebackers looked ready to tear Todd's head off. He could have bolted, but judging by the bulges under the three men's jackets, he didn't expect to get far. He guessed he was meeting the owner of the Porsche.

"I'm Todd Collins." Todd stepped inside the apartment and closed the door.

"Do you know who I am?" the small man asked.

Todd went to say, "The Porsche owner," but decided against it. He thought it best not to antagonize the situation any more than he had already. He shook his head, finding that his vocal chords had failed him.

"Good. That makes things simpler. It's probably not a good idea that you do. It's only important that I know who you are. Understand?"

Todd nodded.

"I bet you're wishing you'd left your insurance details now, aren't you?" the small man said.

"I can make up for it. I can pay."

The small man held up a hand and shook his head. "It's far too late for that." He looked Todd up and down. "Besides, I doubt you could afford to pay. The damage is incidental, but the consequences of your misdemeanor have been severe. Put the newspaper down."

Todd, confused at first, hesitated before doing as instructed. He placed the newspaper on the chipped coffee table. The small man separated the newspaper from the supplements and opened it out. He tapped the front page with the back of his hand.

"See what you've done."

Todd glanced at the headline: DRUG DEALER BUSTED DURING ROUTINE TRAFFIC STOP.

"The car you hit belongs to an employee of mine. Driving home the other night, he was pulled over for a busted headlight. The cops discovered two kilos of cocaine in his possession. He's in a lot of trouble and I'm minus an employee, not to mention a lot of money. Do you see now? Do you see what you've done and why it has led us to your door?"

"I'm sorry."

"That's not important."

"I didn't know."

"I wouldn't expect you to know. But I've lost a valuable employee who had a job to do. Now he can't do it. This is where you come in." The small man stabbed a finger in Todd's direction.

Todd's stomach twitched. He didn't like what was coming. He knew it was retribution for what he'd done, but it wasn't the kind he wanted. Points on his license and a fine he could accept. He'd even take a beating. But the small man's kind of retribution filled Todd with dread.

"Me?" Todd stammered.

"Yes. You'll have to fill in."

The linebackers wrinkled their noses. They knew Todd wasn't the right man for the job and he agreed with them.

"What do you want me to do?"

The small man beamed. "That's the attitude. These two said I was making a mistake."

The linebackers frowned.

The small man dug in his pocket and threw a set of keys to Todd. Todd caught them and examined them.

"Those fit a black Jag. You'll find it outside Danko's restaurant in the city. Bring it to me in Oakland."

"When?"

"Oh, I like you. I debated about just beating the crap out of you, but I wanted to give you a chance to make up for your error and you've done that. You've assessed the situation and decided to stand by your mistake. I admire that." The small man stood and dropped a note on Todd's newspaper. "Bring the Jag to me tonight. Addresses are on the paper. See you at midnight."

The black linebacker brushed Todd aside to open the door. It was a petty gesture, but Todd wasn't going to tell him that.

Todd grabbed the small man's arm on his way out. The small man stared at Todd, his look piercing. Todd knew enough not to touch him, but he didn't care. He knew what was being asked of him was illegal. He just needed to know how illegal.

"Will I find drugs in that car?" Todd demanded.

The linebackers stiffened. The small man nodded at his arm. Todd released his grasp.

"Unfortunately, you don't have a choice, Todd," the small man said, his tone barbed. "Be at the Oakland address at midnight."

* * *

Todd resorted to public transportation to get him into San Francisco, seeing as the linebackers had finished off the Accord. He was looking at a couple of thousand to replace the tires and windshield. It was cheaper to get another car.

A combination of BART, MUNI and good old-fashioned walking brought him out on the corner of Bush and Powell. Danko's was classy and unique for the city. It had its own parking lot. Strictly, it wasn't a parking lot. To the right of the restaurant was a dead end alley, which had been cordoned off to make a parking lot. Two valets protected it. They looked as if they were relations of the small man's linebackers. Obviously, the small man was making Todd work hard to make up for the fender bender. It wasn't going to be easy, but it was doable.

He breezed on by the restaurant, counting his steps, then turned right at the next block onto Powell. He turned right at the next cross street and counted his steps again. When he counted eighty-seven, he stopped in front of a narrow apartment block that looked squeezed by its neighbors. The door was locked, but there was a buzzer entry system. Todd pressed the first one his finger fell on.

"Yes," a woman answered.

"Pizza delivery," Todd said.

"We didn't order any pizza," she barked.

"Sorry, is this 3A?"

"No, 4A, moron."

"Sorry. Can you buzz me in?"

She growled and the door clicked.

Todd let himself in and bounded up the first flight of stairs. The good news, as he had hoped, was the landing window opened out onto the restaurant's alley parking lot. The bad news was that there were no fire escapes. They were all on the front of the building. He flicked the safety latches and slid the window open. Surprisingly, it opened with ease.

One of the valets trotted up the alley to collect a Range Rover. Todd waited until the SUV and owner were reunited, then he climbed onto the ledge and jumped out. He connected hard with the ground. Electricity crackled through his legs, intensifying in his groin. He bit back a scream and crumpled onto his knees. The valets didn't notice him. They were too busy hustling for a tip. Todd crawled behind the nearest car to survey the lot.

Todd had a new problem. There were two black Jags in the parking lot, one a XK8, the other an S-type. The small man had told him to pick up a black Jag, but he hadn't told him the model or license number. He fumbled in his pocket for the keys. He aimed the remote in the direction of both cars and pressed the unlock button. The S-type chirped and blinked its lights. The valets whipped around at the noise. Todd burst out of the shadows, charging for the Jag. The valets did likewise. Todd was lucky on two counts. First, the valets were big, but not fast, and second, he was closer.

He reached the car, dived in front of the wheel and gunned the engine, all before the valets were halfway to him. He cranked the steering and hit the gas. The Jag leapt forward, smearing its fender across the back of a Lincoln Navigator, setting off its alarm. The Jag bounced off another car before he gained control.

One of the valets raced back to the gates while the other blocked the alley with his body. He made himself wide by crouching and splaying out his arms. If they were playing chicken, Todd knew he had the upper hand and floored the gas.

"Time to jump, buddy," Todd said, grinning.

Todd's grin slipped when he realized the second before he hit the guy that the valet wasn't going anywhere. He smashed into the windshield and disappeared over the roof.

The remaining valet had closed the gates, but hadn't locked them and Todd blasted them open. They slammed back against the side of the restaurant, busting its neon sign. Todd jumped on the brakes to prevent the Jag from slamming into the apartment block opposite. Traffic slithered to a screaming halt and he floored the gas pedal, fishtailing down the street and jumping the first red light he hit.

His heart out-revved the S-type. Neat adrenaline raced through his veins and sweat poured off him. Heading towards the Bay Bridge, his pipe wrench grip on the steering wheel softened and his foot eased off the gas.

He laughed. His panic and fear changed into exhilaration and excitement. His crime-fueled buzz was hard to deny. He liked being a criminal. It beat stacking boxes.

* * *

The drop off point was in Oakland's warehouse district, near the rejuvenated Jack London Square, except the address wasn't in the fancier end of the neighborhood. Todd pulled up in front of a white-washed building that was in desperate need of a fresh coat. The building had an address, but no sign giving any clues as to its business.

Todd got out of the Jag and banged on the rollup door. Before he was finished banging, the door retracted. He hopped back into the S-type and drove the car in.

The warehouse's interior was in marginally better condition than the exterior, but was well lit. The place was barren, except for a scattered collection of Snap-On tool chests and half a dozen car lifts. Cars Todd couldn't afford occupied the lifts. The small man stood in the middle of the warehouse floor with the familiar linebackers and a few new friends. Todd parked and got out.

"Christ! What the hell have you been up to?" The small man examined the busted headlight and scarred paintwork. "Do you do this to all the cars you drive, or just mine?"

The rollup door closed with a bang. The noise echoed off the walls.

"It wasn't easy getting the car out. You didn't say anything about stealing it."

"I didn't say anything about smashing it up either. Or were you just trying to impress me?"

"Sorry." Todd didn't know what else to say.

The small man waved the issue aside. "Don't worry, I just wanted the car back. The condition is unimportant. Dalton, park that thing."

The black linebacker shifted the Jag over to the lifts and the rest of the hired help set about stripping the car.

"Are we square? Can I go?" Todd sounded tired, more tired than he felt.

"Not yet." The small man patted Todd on the shoulder. "You're close. There's just one more thing before accounts are squared away. Vasquez, give him the keys."

The Hispanic linebacker tossed a set of keys to Todd and he caught them.

"Those fit that Lexus over there. I want you to drive it to Dallas."

"Texas?"

"The one and only. Don't look so worried. This job is a lot easier than the last one. All you have to do is drop it off at Ruskin's. It's a dealership. Your contact is Charlie Ruskin. Then you're done and our business is concluded."

"That's a good two day drive. I can't do that. I have a job."

The small man's irritation evaporated his grin. He yanked out an automatic pistol and jammed it in Todd's face. "You drive or you die. Your choice. You've cost me a lot of money and I think I've been damn charitable giving you this chance to redeem yourself.

So what's it to be?" He snapped the safety off the pistol.

"Drive," Todd managed.

"Good. You said two days, but I'm going to be generous. You have three days to get this car to Texas."

The preamble was over. A minute later, he was on the road, Texas bound. The euphoria he felt stealing the Jag seeped away with the prospect of the boring drive ahead of him. The small man had really screwed him this time. He'd given him a schedule that meant no time to pack any clothes or leave a message. He hit the road as he was dressed. He couldn't blame the small man too much. If he'd done the right thing in the first place, he wouldn't be on I-580 now.

"You're a dumb, dumb man, Todd," he said to himself and turned the radio up.

* * *

The miles passed swiftly at that time of night, but compared to the length of the drive, he seemed to be crawling. Fatigue got to him by the time he reached the California/Arizona state line and he pulled off the highway and slept in the car. The sleep did little to rejuvenate his spirits. The small man's vice grip around his nuts forced him to drive hard. His fellow freeway users received no charity from him. They were on his road and in his way. He flashed his high beams when someone moved into his lane and never conceded an inch to anyone who wanted to merge or change lanes. He didn't stop to eat or drink. He took a piss when he filled up with gas. His bad mood lasted as far as New Mexico.

Evening was descending and he was driving into another night. His stale breath cloyed at the back of his throat to the extent that he could taste its noxious odor. His BO was so ripe that its stench permeated the inside of his skull. He'd washed up as best he could in a gas station restroom, but his clothes were rancid. He pulled off at Gallup and raided a Wal-Mart for a change of under shorts and a couple of tee shirts. At a diner that boasted all-day breakfasts, he changed into his fresh clothes in the restroom and tossed the dirty ones in their trash. He decided to eat there too. Having only eaten his own stomach acid along with the junk food he'd gotten from gas stations, their sausage and egg skillet tasted like heaven at nine in the evening. He couldn't help but groan with pleasure with every swallow of coffee. He drooled over their pies, but resisted. He wanted to get on the road again. He'd spent too long indulging himself. Besides, on a different day under different circumstances, this meal would have rated only a couple steps above pet food.

He hit the roads in good spirits, which improved the closer he got to the Texas state line. Sure, he'd screwed himself with the small man, but that would soon end. Texas was a big state but he'd be in Dallas by this time tomorrow and then he'd be a free man again. It didn't matter that he didn't have any way of getting back to the Bay Area. All that mattered was that he would be out from under the small man and wouldn't that first inhale of air taste sweet? Forgetting himself, he took in a practice breath. It jolted him from his reverie.

The Lexus' interior stunk with his odor. He wouldn't be surprised if it had impregnated the vehicle linings and leather seats. If Ruskin's couldn't get it out, the small man would exact his wrath.

Sweat, hot and persistent, leaked out from under his arms and down his spine, ruining his fresh clothes. The hairs on the back of his neck bristled and gooseflesh broke out underneath it. *Payback*, he thought. Delivering this car was payback for screwing over the small man. One of the small man's lieutenants had been taken down by Todd's mistake. Stealing one car and transporting another seemed like a small price to pay for the potential loss in revenue he'd caused and the subsequent heat provided by a police investigation as a result. It didn't make sense. It wasn't enough. The small man wouldn't let him get off this easily. What Todd had done as payback hardly measured a pound of flesh. There had to be more.

He sniffed the car's rank air again. It didn't smell right. He powered down the windows for twenty minutes and let the night air flood in and wash the stink away. When he powered the windows back up, he sniffed again. The smell was still there, just as pungent and persistent and it didn't smell like sweat or bad breath.

His hands trembled as a thought punctured his brain. He fought to keep them steady. At the first off-ramp, he pulled off I-40 and drove along some poorly maintained county road until he found an abandoned strip mall. He parked around back out of view of passersby. He popped the trunk and walked to the rear of the vehicle.

He didn't have to guess at what he'd find. The stench rammed a fist through the sweet night air.

Shrink-wrapped in plastic was the contorted shape of a man. The corpse's bulging eyes and tongue pressed against the tight plastic. Decomposition had set about its merry work and the body had bloated, stretching the plastic beyond the breaking point. The plastic seams had snapped in several places letting out the stink. Even through the distortions, Todd recognized the dead man from his picture in the newspaper. He was the Porsche owner the cops had picked up after Todd had hit his car.

Todd sighed. The small man wasn't going to let this slide. Todd should have seen the setup. Stealing the Jag was merely a ploy to keep him busy while the small man took care of the Porsche driver. The cops would know the Porsche driver worked for the small man and he couldn't let a loose end like that exist without cutting it off. The cops didn't know about Todd, but he was another loose end that needed trimming.

He wondered how this was supposed to go down. Had the small man set up a tit-for-tat sting? What and who was waiting for him in Dallas? The cops? Thugs? No one? For all he knew, Ruskin's dealership had nothing to do with the small man. Maybe the dealership was a name plucked from the Yellow Pages purely as a carrot for Todd to follow while the cops picked him up along the way.

Todd could have been angry, but he smiled instead. Credit where credit was due. The small man had almost put one over on him. Todd had been eager to believe he could climb out of the hole he found himself in and was willing to accept any crap the small man wanted to feed him. It had almost worked. He guessed highway cops were supposed to pick him up long before he reached the Lone Star state. Instead, luck, in its twisted and cruel form, had intervened. He was still in the game. He might just get away with it. He slammed the trunk down on the body. There was a lot to do.

Todd rejoined the I-40. He had to get rid of the body and car. The car had to be on the hot list, but he couldn't dump it—not just yet. He consulted the maps he'd picked up in a gas station, then drove to Santa Rosa. It was a small town with an infrastructure just big enough to swallow up a stranger.

He pulled off at the freeway exit and trawled the downtown. He parked across the street from a chain motel he had no intention of staying at. He looked for security cameras in the parking lot. He didn't see any. It wasn't surprising. This was the New Mexico equivalent of Green Acres. Crime just didn't happen here. He scanned the rows of docile vehicles for a Lexus and found none. It would have been nice, but it wasn't important. Any vehicle would do. He dropped to his knees behind a rental car with Texas plates, jerked out his penknife blade and unscrewed the license plate. Local plates were all he wanted. The cops would be looking for a Lexus with California plates. Okay, it wasn't perfect. An inquisitive cop would see through that, even expect that, but it was the best he could do under the circumstances. Stealing from a rental car bought him some additional time too. The renters wouldn't give the missing plate a second thought, not like if it had belonged to their own personal vehicle. Who would care? The renters wouldn't. They wouldn't know the license plate number even if Todd parked next to them. It was flawed, but close enough for government work.

Keeping to the shadows, Todd scurried back to the Lexus and swapped plates at a diner a couple of miles away. He stopped for coffee and time to think. Disposing of the body had to be done right. He couldn't be rash. That would get him caught. No, he wouldn't dump the corpse tonight. Besides not having any tools, he didn't know where to dump the body. He needed somewhere remote, not only for today but for the next decade. No, he'd sleep tonight, tool up in the morning, spend the rest of the day finding a burial site and dig a deep dark hole tomorrow night. He paid his check and there was a confident bounce to his step on the way out.

He could have driven back to the motel where he'd lifted the license plates, but he decided against it. Fate didn't need tempting. He picked up the freeway again. He didn't have to be careful about the roads he used now. To the outside world, he was a Texas native in his Texas-bought Lexus, as long as they didn't look too closely.

He fancied staying the night in town for no good reason other than he liked the idea of sleeping in a bed. It sounded like a good plan. He settled into his drive. He switched on the radio for the first time and searched for a radio station that didn't play country or

Mexican music. He couldn't find one and settled for country. He racked up the miles listening to people having the kinds of troubles Todd only wished he had.

"You think that's bad," he said to the hapless cowboy lamenting the loss of his girl. "You should walk a mile in my shoes."

Headlights lit up the Lexus from behind and Todd deflected his rearview mirror to shield his eyes. He'd thought it was some jerk who didn't know when to dip his high beams until he recognized the familiar outline of a police car. He hadn't seen them, not that he'd been keeping an eye out. He'd been playing it safe, keeping to the speed limit and using his turn signals. He shouldn't have registered on anyone's radar. All the spit in his mouth escaped to somewhere safe.

Now he wished he'd dumped the body back in Santa Rosa. He'd take the stint for grand theft auto and not bitch about it, but he didn't want to go down for the body too. Not that it would ever come to that. The small man would have connections. Todd would never see the inside of a courtroom. He held his breath, waiting for the light bar to burst into life and bathe him in red and blue.

But the lights never came.

The state troopers were checking the license plate with the one on the hot car list. It wouldn't match up. He thanked God that he'd switched the plates already.

"I'm not the person you're looking for," he murmured at the car reflected in his rearview mirror. "Don't stop me. Go by."

As if by magic, the troopers granted his request. The driver killed the high beams and sped past.

Todd realized a mammoth breath he'd been holding. That was too close for comfort. Time to get off the road for the night.

He pulled off at Tucumcari and checked into a motel. He had to show ID, but paid cash and hoped that wouldn't leave a trail for the small man or anyone else to find.

"No one pays cash these days," the sleepy-eyed clerk said.

Todd smiled. "Never a lender or borrower be."

The clerk shrugged, handed Todd a cardkey and went back to the TV he had playing behind him.

Todd found his room and slept the sleep of the innocent, so

much so, he didn't wake until housekeeping knocked on the door. It was after eleven. He couldn't remember the last time he'd slept that well. He was sure this was a sign. A sign of what though?

He picked up a late breakfast at a drive-thru burger joint and tracked down the nearest hardware store. The Lexus stood out next to all the pickups, but there wasn't a lot he could do about that. He trawled the aisles with his cart and filled it with a pick and shovel and bunch of unnecessary crap for cover. The last thing he needed was to be remembered by the staff as the guy who bought a shovel then asked for directions to a large chunk of nowhere. So he made it look like he was a greenhorn handyman who watched too much DIY TV embarking on a landscaping project he couldn't possibly pull off.

Standing in the checkout line, he examined the contents of his wallet. The hotel and this purchase would drain him of most of his cash reserves. He'd have to make some money soon, but that would have to wait until the corpse was in the ground.

He paid and loaded up the Lexus. From his maps, the best place for a drug dealer burial was out at the parklands surrounding Ute Lake State Park. It was an hour or so from Tucumcari using the local highways. After last night's run-in with the state troopers, Todd wanted to avoid the freeways.

He reached the State Park by mid-afternoon. He left the Lexus on the road and explored the areas north of the park on foot. If anyone came snooping, Todd had his cover story. *Sorry, Officer. I drank three cups of coffee and nature took its course. You know how it is when you're miles from anywhere. I had to go somewhere.*

He climbed a small rise and surveyed the land around him. The place defined nothingness. Wildness spread in all directions marred only by the empty roadway he'd traveled. It was stunning to think that the US could still have places as unpopulated and undeveloped as this considering how high property prices were in the Bay Area. Undeveloped or not, it was going to make for a perfect burial site.

Chain link fencing cordoned the land off from road users and signs stated the land was private property, but the land was so vast that the owners would need a herd of security officers to enforce the penalties threatened on the signs.

He didn't see much point in driving off and coming back under the cover of darkness. He busted off the padlock on the gate and drove through and relocked the gates with a padlock he'd brought with him. He picked his gravesite and parked the Lexus out of the view of the roadway. He retrieved the shovel and the pick from the car's trunk and broke ground. Digging a grave wasn't as easy as in the movies. This wasn't Hollywood dirt. The sun-baked ground yielded little to his pick. It bounced off the dirt leaving behind a minor dent in comparison to the effort he exerted. To soften the ground up, he poured all his bottled water onto the dirt. The thirsty earth sucked up every last drop without giving anything back in return. He was in no mood to be screwed over now when he was so close and smashed away at the ground until it finally succumbed.

The sun had long set and the day's heat was waning when he had a person-length hole just under two feet deep. It was a shallow grave fit for a drug dealer. How his blistered and bleeding hands and aching back wished that were true. But two feet wasn't anywhere deep enough. Scavengers would be chewing over the remains in no time. Six feet was too much to ask, but four, that sounded like a reasonable depth to him. It got no easier the deeper he dug. The ground was softer and gave way to his pick and shovel more readily, but it was a damn sight harder to hurl the dirt to the surface from that depth.

When the hole reached chest deep, Todd stopped. He tossed the shovel out of the hole and tried to straighten. His lower back screamed as each vertebrae failed to pop back into place. It took him three attempts to clamber out of the grave. How ironic would it be if he ended up digging his own grave? He imagined the small man would get a kick out of it.

He hefted the plastic-clad corpse from the Lexus. He possessed enough strength to lift the body over the seemingly mile-high trunk lip, but not enough to stop it from rolling out and crashing to the ground. On his knees, he rolled the dead drug dealer to the edge of the grave. He went to give the corpse one final roll when he stopped. He couldn't bury it with the plastic on. It would take forever to decompose. He'd have to remove the drug dealer from his packaging. It was a simple task, but Todd didn't relish it. The stink associated with releasing the three-day-old corpse from its shroud turned his stomach, but it had to be done. He retrieved the box cutter from his purchases and sliced open the plastic. He didn't allow himself time to psyche himself out of doing this. He just dropped to his knees in front of the corpse, stuck the blade in at the head and ran the keen edge all the way down to the feet. There was no finesse or skill to this action and he took no care to avoid cutting the clothes or the body. He held his breath as the stench poured from the rapidly expanding slit. He gagged, but the moment the body was free of the plastic, Todd rolled it into the grave. It struck the bottom of the hole with a satisfying thud.

Fluids rested in the folds of the plastic sheeting. Todd gagged again and he kicked the plastic in with the body. There was no way he was taking that back with him.

The drug dealer's leaking residues galvanized Todd. He snatched up the shovel and thrashed at the freely dug earth, piling it back onto the stinking body. His disgust petered out when he'd filled the grave three-quarters full. After a short break, he piled on the rest of the dirt and smoothed it over. It looked pretty good, even under moonlight.

He fell behind the wheel of the Lexus and drove off the property. Hitting the road, he realized that half his problems were over. He just had to offload the car and he was free. He wondered if the Lexus came with any papers—crooked or straight. He reached over to the glove box and popped it open. A nickel-plated .357 fell out into the passenger side foot well.

Todd slammed on the brakes. The gun slid across the carpeting. He picked it up. *Another present from the small man?* he wondered. He rifled through the glove box's contents. No registration, but there was a cell phone. The phone would come in handy. He switched it on and slipped it into the door pocket.

He examined the revolver. It was loaded and well maintained. He didn't like guns, but like the phone, it would come in handy. "You really want to see me burn, don't you?" he said to the absent small man and returned it to the glove box.

Todd went to pull away but hesitated. His gut churned. Something still wasn't right. It wasn't enough. He felt there was more. Anything less was beneath the small man. The car concealed another unseen surprise. He smelled it as strongly as he had the corpse.

He shined his flashlight under the car. Nothing dangled underneath and he didn't find anything in the engine bay or hidden in the trunk. He turned his focus to the Lexus' interior. Still, nothing. He knew he wasn't wrong. His punishment wasn't over. Kneeling on the ground, he thumped the rear seat in frustration. His fist bounced off the rock hard backseat.

He looked at his fist and the seat. His blow hadn't left a dent. This was a Lexus, a luxury car, providing quality and a refined ride for all its occupants. He felt that in the driver's seat, but not the rear. He examined the seat up close with the flashlight. The seams were machined stitched, but the stitching differed to the rest used in the vehicle.

"Gotcha," Todd said.

With the box cutter, he slit the seams. A cloud of white puffed up through the incision. The powder dusted the black leather. He wiped up the powder on his fingertips and tasted it. The powder tasted bitter with a medicinal kick. Moments later his tongue went numb where the powder had touched. He didn't recognize the taste but he knew what it was—cocaine. He smiled. It was fitting. He had to hand it to the small man. He knew how to twist the blade.

Todd spent the next twenty minutes carefully cutting open the backseat's leather to reveal six bricks of white powder, each weighing around a couple of pounds each. If this coke was supposed to hang him, the small man had just screwed up tying the noose. He'd just made Todd rich. That euphoria passed the moment it arrived. He'd dug himself a big enough hole hitting that Porsche. What kind of shitstorm would he conjure up if he tried to push the small man's dope? He tossed the packets on the roadside, got in the car and left two long tire marks getting the hell away from that accident waiting to happen.

He got a hundred yards. He left an equally impressive pair of tire marks stopping the Lexus. He couldn't leave all that coke on the highway. Like the gun, it was useful. Not to sell of course, but useful in other ways. That amount could be a valuable bargaining chip. He backed the Lexus up and stored the cocaine in the trunk with all the landscaping equipment.

He'd been on the road twenty minutes when the phone rang. He'd forgotten that he'd left it on. He answered it.

"There you are," said the small man. Todd almost choked on the sarcasm. "I would have thought you'd have dropped the car off by now. I was frightened you'd fallen off the radar."

"Yeah, well, I ran into a couple of problems."

"Tell me about them."

"Nothing to tell seeing as you were the cause."

The small man laughed. "So you found my gifts."

"Some quite expensive."

"I know."

"Well, none of them were to my taste, so I gave them away."

"You shouldn't have done that. I would have taken them back."

"Too late now. They're all gone. No one will ever find them."

"I've misjudged you. You have an aptitude for this work. You've proven to be much smarter than I expected."

"Yeah, I know." Todd powered down the window and tossed the phone into the night. "And I'm getting smarter all the time."

PART TWO
DETOUR

Todd's aching muscles woke him. Every one of them expressed their annoyance at their mistreatment and now exacted their revenge. He groaned when he rolled out of his motel bed. He'd checked himself in when he realized he didn't have to run anymore.

He schlepped over to the bathroom and stood under a shower for far too long. While the hot water picked away at his knotted muscles, he thought about the small man. This distracted him from the pain in his overworked body. He recalled the small man's final words before he tossed the cell phone out of the Lexus' window.

"You have an aptitude for this work."

Todd found it hard to disagree with this. Less than a week ago, he was working a dead end job, going nowhere with his boring and annoying life, but now, who knew? His life was a blank sheet. He could do anything. He could relocate. Start afresh. Reinvent himself. He still had to get a few things out of the way first, namely the coke, the car and the gun. The gun was easy. There were plenty of storm drains. He fancied trading the Lexus in. That would rectify his pitiful money situation for the moment. The coke. That was the tricky one. He'd vacillated over that one all during the drive and through the night. He could flush that shit down the drain or go into business for himself. One was a smart idea and the other was the worst known to man. There was an even more appealing idea. Use the coke to stick it to the small man. Yeah, he liked that. But that didn't have to happen overnight. Revenge took time. He needed to get the measure of his opposition. At this point, he didn't know jack about the small man and that was like taking a ripe banana to a gunfight. No, the coke wouldn't get dumped down a drain or sucked up a nose. It would rest awhile.

He'd holed up in a place called Grassmore, a small town thirty minutes east of the New Mexico/Texas border. He checked out of the motel and drove into town where he breakfasted at a down-on-its-luck diner that served pretty decent food. He bought a cheap backpack at a drugstore and deposited the six packets of cocaine inside it. The pack weighed more than its twelve-pound plus cargo when he walked into the bus station with it slung over his shoulder. He expected everyone to instantly know what he was carrying on him. He nodded to the cop standing sentry at the main entrance to the station. The cop gave him scant regard. Todd found the lockers and stuffed the backpack in one. The locker slammed shut with a satisfying bang. He pocketed the locker key and slipped out of the station's side door.

That out of the way, it was time to say goodbye to his faithful steed, the Lexus. He tore a page out of the yellow pages listing dealerships and drove out to them. They all looked to be respectable. A respectable dealer wouldn't touch the car, especially with a shredded rear seat.

He needed a non-respectable dealer, but where would he find one? On the rough side of town? He wouldn't know the rough side of town if it bit him on the ass. He picked up a local newspaper and flicked through the pages. The news loved to dish the dirt and he found it. The Texan, a bar on the outskirts of town, had been busted again after two roughnecks took a bar fight to the next level. The winner of the battle was facing a manslaughter charge. The newspaper alluded to drug dealing and other crimes too heinous to mention. It sounded like the perfect place to move a hot car, as long as no one broke a pool cue over his head.

The Texan didn't reach simmer until eight o'clock that night, when a motley crew filed in to drown their sorrows. Todd struck up a couple of dead end conversations at the bar at the cost of a couple of drinks. His stranger status closed verbal doors.

His latest shunning drew the attention of the bartender. He'd been watching her bartending prowess all night. She worked the bar with effortless efficiency and kept the clientele in check. Todd developed a large measure of respect for her, but this respect wasn't mutual judging by the glare she shot him. They made eye contact and she wandered over to him.

Todd cast an appreciating glance over her. He guessed she was in her late-forties and she was clinging on to her good looks and figure by a thread. She'd thickened in the waist and her sun-damaged skin could never be repaired, but she worked her remaining assets. Her bust was still to die for. She sported a number of tattoos on her wrists, biceps and shoulder blades and they looked to have adorned her skin long before tattoos proved to be en vogue with the pretty young things. Todd found her personality her most attractive trait. She exuded strength and self-assurance. She must have been a dynamite package in her day.

"Looking for a friend?" she asked in a tone that offered little friendliness.

"What makes you say that?"

"You've bought just about every idiot in here a drink."

"Is that a problem?"

"It can be, if you're buying those drinks for the wrong reasons."

"I'm just after a little help."

Some guy well on his way to drunkdom although the clock had yet to chime ten yelled out from three stools down, "Ginger, leave lover boy alone. I need a beer."

"And you can wait for it," Ginger barked back without taking her eyes off Todd.

The drunk looked wounded and sat back down. His drinking buddy patted him on the shoulder to console him.

"So why don't you tell me what you need?"

"I want to sell my car. I'm not local, I'm passing through and I wanted the name of a dealer who wouldn't stiff me. Know anyone?" Todd threw in a smile to sweeten the deal.

He failed to melt Ginger's heart.

"If you're passing through, aren't you going to need that car?"

No pulling the wool over Ginger's eyes, but Todd had it covered.

He'd spent the day coming up with cover stories. "The thing is costing me too much money. I'm working on a budget these days."

"Is that right?"

Todd nodded and tried the smile again with no success.

"I'm sure any dealer in town can help you out." She paused for effect. "Unless there's a reason why you can't go to any dealer."

Todd noticed how green her eyes were. Amber flecks acted as contrast to bring the green out even more. She noticed him looking at her eyes and not her "go to" tits. That seemed to smooth the edges a bit.

"You're right, I can't go to just anyone. I'm ducking a bad relationship and the loan company still has dibs on the car. You know how those bastards can be when you're down on your luck. I'm looking for someone that's not too fussy about paperwork." Todd paused for dramatic effect this time, hoping for a little sympathy. "Can you hook me up?"

Ginger scrutinized him with a piercing stare that cut through bullshit at fifty paces.

"You know what I think?" she said.

"No. What do you think?"

"I think you're a cop."

If only she knew the truth. Todd shook his head in protest, but she ignored this and plowed on.

"This place has a bad reputation and you sons of bitches want to find any excuse to shut me down, regardless whether you have to invent one or not."

"Look, honestly, I'm not a cop."

"I don't care. You're not welcome. Get out."

Todd pleaded his innocence again until Ginger reached under the bar for a small Billy club. This was coupled with a significant number of supportive patrons rising from their seats. He raised his hands in surrender and backed away towards the exit. He made it unmolested and broke into a jog when he felt the hot night air close its arms around him. Even though no one followed him out, he didn't slow up until he reached the Lexus. He got behind the wheel and gunned the engine.

Before he could leave a trail of dirt, a young Hispanic guy blocked his path. Unlike Ginger and many of her compadres, this guy possessed the build of a twelve-inch ruler viewed edge on. If he wanted to tussle, Todd fancied his chances.

Seeing Todd hesitate, the kid raced to the passenger side and jumped into the seat next to him. "I heard what you said."

"Which was what?" Todd asked.

"You want someone to take this car."

Todd mulled over Ginger's assumption. The cops were looking to shut the Texan down and didn't care how they did it. Entrapment seemed like a minor twisting of the law and this kid could be a cop. Ginger may have sized him up all wrong, but he had the measure of this kid. He wasn't a cop on his first undercover job. He could trust him.

"You know someone?"

"Yeah. Is it worth something to you?"

"Of course. Who?"

"Larry Vandrel. He'll take care of you."

The kid rattled off directions, which seemed simple enough to follow to Todd. He thanked the kid and pressed a twenty into the kid's hand when he shook it. It wasn't much of a thank you, but it satisfied the kid and he returned to the Texan's loving embrace.

The kid's directions took Todd out of town and past the residential areas into the desert. Vandrel had to be the real deal. The warehouse he worked out of, formerly an aircraft hangar at a disused landing strip, possessed no sign—just a security light spraying a cone of light in the darkness.

Todd pulled up next to a grime-encrusted tow truck and went up to the hangar doors. He thought he heard voices, but realized it was a radio playing. He leaned on one of the doors and slid it back. A good ole boy sporting bib overalls and a shotgun appeared from behind a car lift.

"Can I help you, son?"

Neither the gun nor the good ole boy's placid tone bothered Todd. He was beginning to take this kind of treatment in stride. "I'm looking for Larry Vandrel."

"You've found him."

"They tell me you take trade-ins."

This explanation failed to prompt Vandrel to lower his shotgun.

He did take a number of measured steps to take him within range of Todd. If he set off the shotgun, it would punch a hole the size of a melon in Todd's chest. "And who exactly is *they*?"

"Some Hispanic kid at the Texan."

"This Mex got a name?"

"I didn't ask and he didn't tell."

"I don't like unannounced arrivals. You should have made an appointment."

"Sorry, I didn't get your phone number."

Vandrel dropped the shotgun's muzzle to his side. "Let's see what you've got."

He brushed by Todd and looked over the Lexus. The security light failed to bring out the Lexus' best and he instructed Todd to bring the sedan inside the hangar. Vandrel hit a switch and a bank of fluorescent lights flooded the hangar. The light revealed rows and rows of vehicles in various states of disrepair. There looked to be a spray booth in the far corner.

Vandrel surveyed the Lexus, circling the car like he was examining an antique with his nose inches from the paintwork and his hands tucked behind him with the shotgun in his grasp. After he circled the Lexus three times, he straightened and faced Todd.

"Don't no one buy American these days?"

"I think Lexuses are made in the US."

"Don't give me that. A Jap car is a Jap car wherever it's built."

Todd let the subject of foreign trade drop. A heated debate could affect the final price.

Vandrel opened the rear passenger door and peered in at the shredded backseat. He paused in contemplation before slamming the door shut.

"So what's the story, son? Why have you driven all the way out to me?"

Todd fed him the same line he'd spooned to Ginger about the bad breakup and the repo man. Vandrel mulled the lie over.

"Finance companies. They're your friends when you're riding high and the enemy when you're on the skids," Vandrel said.

"Ain't that the truth."

"And the backseat?"

"Vandals. The bastards broke in and tore it up."

"They didn't go to town on it."

"They were probably disturbed in the act. I suppose I should count myself lucky."

"That you should. Anyway, it's getting late and I still have things to do. Let's talk numbers. Blue book on this is around twenty grand, even with the torn up backseat," he began.

Todd failed to hide his delight. Twenty grand would go a long way. It was the stuff that fresh starts were made from.

"But I'll give you five hundred," Vandrel finished.

Vandrel's punch line forced a gasp out of Todd. He should have known this wasn't going to be easy.

"If you're not interested, why don't you say, instead of wasting your time and mine?" Todd hadn't intended on unleashing such a venom-filled response, but Vandrel shouldn't have jerked him around. He brushed by the guy to get to the driver's door, but Vandrel blocked his path with the shotgun.

"Son, this car is worth five hundred bucks because it comes with twenty grand's worth of trouble attached to it. Correct me if I'm wrong."

Todd invoked his Fifth Amendment right and said nothing.

"I didn't think so," Vandrel said and lowered the gun. "Have you got papers for this vehicle?"

"No."

"Is there anybody looking for it?"

"Not in this state."

"That's good. That's just tacked on a couple of hundred."

Seven hundred bucks. That wasn't worth wiping his ass on.

"So what's the real story on this?" Vandrel nodded in the direction of the Lexus.

Todd didn't see much point in bullshitting. Vandrel had it all worked out except for the finer details.

"As far as I know, the car's stolen and I was supposed to deliver it to Dallas."

"Dallas? I don't know if you've noticed, but you're a half a day's drive from there. What changed?"

"Circumstances."

"Circumstances might just bite me just as hard as they've bitten you. I think I'll take that two hundred back."

"Back to five hundred then?"

Vandrel nodded. "I'll ask again. What's with the backseat?"

"An unexpected bonus for my time. It's gone. You don't have to know about it."

"But it sounds like I should worry about it. I'm getting the idea that I should keep my five hundred and let you be on your way."

Funny what a few minutes did. The five hundred deal had insulted Todd. Now he lamented its loss like an old friend. "If that's the way you want to play it, fine. I'll take my business elsewhere."

"Now, then, cool your heels, son. What's your name?"

"Todd."

"Todd, I like you. Yeah, you can give me that look, but it's true. You're a straight shooter and I appreciate that. I deal with a lot of scum. Not that that bothers me, mind. It comes with the territory. I find it refreshing to find someone who doesn't see bullshit as necessary as air. I'll tell you what. I'll give you ten grand for the Lexus. I know that's not what you were hoping for but you're not in a position to bargain. You're in a hole and me throwing you a line does me no favors unless you do something for me in return. Ten grand is good money, you've got to agree?"

Todd did agree. In all honesty, he was expecting a couple of grand and hoping for five. Ten, although not as pleasing to the ear as twenty, still possessed a natural beauty he could admire. But it also seemed generous to the point that it gave Todd pause. There was something coming and he speeded its arrival.

"Ten grand is very generous, considering the situation," Todd replied.

"Yes, well, the money isn't just for the vehicle."

"No?"

"No. You're going to have to do a job for me first."

"What job?"

* * *

As mayors went, Lyle Moran was no Rudy Giuliani. Then again, Dumont was no New York City. Four thousand souls called Dumont home and the city clung to its incorporated status by its fingertips thanks to Moran. The town was so small, his mayoral status was a part-time position. Most of the city's services were subbed out to county agencies. Moran earned an income from his hardware store and after a hard day's graft from selling two by fours and chainsaws, Dumont's residents could find their mayor at the Yellow Rose tavern. Despite this, Moran was a popular figure. He swapped near-the-knuckle jokes, slapped backs and on occasion, the behinds of women a decade beyond their prime and everyone loved him for it. Lyle Moran was the people's man, albeit a good couple of steps out of stride with the big city world. Being Dumont's mayor wasn't a sign of civic duty but a popularity contest and Moran won hands down.

Todd came up with this assessment after shadowing Moran for a day and a half in a pickup he'd gotten from Vandrel. He'd done a pretty good job fitting in. The unrelenting sun had darkened his skin and the absence of air-conditioning left a permanent shine of sweat. He disguised his stranger factor further by bunking down at Vandrel's chop shop instead of checking into a motel. He'd even managed to mimic the local accent. It was far from perfect. People knew he wasn't local but guessed he was from the vicinity. He wouldn't have gone to all this effort if the job Vandrel had given him had been of the wham, bam, thank you ma'am variety.

That was the easy part. The tough part was getting close enough to Moran to clean out his safe. Vandrel had been vague as to the reasons why he wanted Todd to rob Moran. Todd couldn't see how this man was connected to Vandrel and he didn't care too much either. He just wanted the ten grand Vandrel had promised him.

Dusk was handing over the reins to night and the Yellow Rose had been well patronized since quitting time. Country western music leaked from an aging boom box. Two ceiling fans stirred the hot air, failing to cool it. But no one seemed to mind the heat as long as Grady, the Yellow Rose's owner, kept supplying the beer.

Todd had concealed himself in the shadows. He was on his third bottle of Bud Lite and cleaning the bottom of a chili bowl. He wouldn't have credited Grady with the ability to come up with good Tex-Mex, but he pulled it off.

He'd done enough surveillance. It was time to make contact. He drained the Bud and approached the bar. He stood behind Moran and the three other guys he was shooting the breeze with. There was a gap at the bar rail for him to stand at, but he wanted to be noticed.

Moran, heavy from riding a barstool too often, felt Todd's presence at his shoulder and turned. He wiped back his thick graying hair, which had slipped across his forehead. "Can I help you?"

"No, I'm just after a replacement," Todd said and held up his empty bottle.

"I don't know you, do I?"

"No reason you should."

Grady acknowledged Todd's request and reached for a replacement.

"You could argue that I do have a reason."

"Why argue? It's too hot to argue."

Moran liked that one and laughed. Moran's drinking buddies laughed too.

"You're right. No reason to argue."

Grady handed over the beer to Todd. Todd reached for his wallet and fiddled with the bills.

"I've got this," Moran announced.

"You don't have to do that," Todd countered.

"I think it's only fair that the mayor buy everyone in town a beer."

"You're talking to the honorable Lyle Moran," one of Moran's buddies said.

"You're the mayor?"

"Three terms and counting," Moran said.

"That's very generous of you."

"Not really, that's how I get re-elected."

"I like a politician who's a straight shooter," Todd said and held up his beer to Moran.

This got another round of laughs from Moran and the boys.

Moran swiveled on his barstool to face Todd full on. He smiled, but his cool stare examined Todd with snake-like intensity. "Now that we've established who I am, who are you?"

Todd stuck a hand in Moran's direction. "Todd Collins."

Todd shook hands with Moran. His drinking buddies introduced themselves as Charles "Chuck" Baker, Theo Masterson and J. G. Thorpe.

"Am I buying Dumont's latest voter a beer?"

"Sadly, no, I'm just passing through."

"Then I've got a good mind to ask for that beer back," Moran joked.

Laughs came fast and easy after that. Todd fell into a rhythm with Moran and his buddies. After twenty minutes, he was parked on a barstool next to them. He trotted out his cover story he'd spent the day inventing and Moran and company bought it as gospel. It didn't take long for Moran's examining stare to recede. This gave Todd confidence to keep pushing with his cover story, but he kept it to the right side of cockiness. Moran might be on Todd's side now, but his radar would be scanning for slipups.

Last call came and Todd eased himself off his barstool. The combination of too much beer and heat that squeezed the sweat out of him left him lightheaded when he took his first steps.

"Thanks for your hospitality and I hope our paths cross again," he said.

"Where do you think you're going?" Moran asked.

"It's closing time."

"For the unfavored," Chuck remarked.

"Do you play poker?" Moran asked.

"Sure do."

"Then you're welcome to join us."

While Grady closed up, Moran led everyone to a back room filled with cleaning products and a card table at its center. They settled into a five-handed game of stud poker. Todd feared these guys were scamming him, but after ten minutes, he realized that not even card sharks played this badly. Todd could have cleaned them out, but he wasn't here for that. He followed their lead and lost enough hands to keep the game square.

In some respects, this was a high-powered game. Chuck ran a real estate agency, although Todd couldn't imagine he made much money at it in Dumont. J. G. doubled as the head of the Chamber of Commerce and owned a market on Main Street. Thorpe acted as city clerk while also being a practicing attorney. The game was an excuse to shoot the breeze. They talked about life and business. They probed Todd on his reasons for being in Dumont and he fed them more of his cover story about working his way back to Oklahoma.

"Where were you looking to pick up work?" Moran asked, dealing fresh cards out for a new hand.

"Dallas."

"Have you thought of staying on around here for a spell?"

"No offense, but I'm not sure your town can spare it."

"Oh, you'd be surprised. We can rustle up something to put a young man to work. Can't we, boys?"

A chorus of approval followed.

"If you've got work then I'm happy to do it—whatever it is."

"Good. Then come by the hardware store in the morning. Say nine?"

Todd smiled. He'd hooked Moran. "Nine it is."

* * *

"You don't look any worse for wear," Moran said when Todd walked into Moran's Hardware. "Youth is kind to the young."

Todd nodded, careful not to disturb the hangover skulking in the recesses of his skull. Moran could decry the virtues of youth, but he looked real sharp for someone who had put away the amount of booze that he had the previous night, not to mention that Moran's Hardware had been open since seven. The guy couldn't have had more than four hours sleep. Todd leaned against the checkout counter from where Moran piloted a cash register with no customers.

"Fighting fit and raring to go?" Moran asked.

"Sure am. What do you want me to do for you?" Todd smiled and his face ached.

"Not for me—not directly, leastways. Chuck's all ready for you."

"Chuck?"

"Yeah, I talked it over with him after the game. He's at his most persuadable about then. He gets real charitable when he's down a hundred bucks and full of bourbon."

Todd masked his disappointment well. His plan had just gone to the wall. He'd expected to work alongside Moran and when he had the man's confidence, he'd reward him by cracking his safe, just as Vandrel wanted. Time to switch to Plan B, which he'd put into action as soon as he thought of it.

"Thanks, Lyle. I really appreciate it." Todd did well to keep the sarcasm out.

"Don't thank me. Chuck's the one paying you."

Todd returned to his pickup parked next to Moran's Cadillac CTS. *Not a bad set of wheels for this neck of the woods*, he thought and pulled out of the parking lot. He checked his rearview and the reflected image of Moran's Hardware without a customer in sight. *How do you make your money, Lyle?*

Chuck's realty business wasn't hard to find. Nothing was hard to find in Dumont. Todd parked and walked in. Chuck's offices were small, taking up one half of a commercial unit shared with a coin laundry. Pictures of unsold properties hung in the window and for the most part, they'd always hang in the window. The office furniture, which included a secretary, dated back to the 80's.

Chuck looked how Todd felt, but Chuck put on a good front and was all smiles and bonhomie. He sat Todd down with a much-needed cup of coffee.

"Thanks for the job, Chuck."

"Don't thank me yet. You don't know what it is." He laughed his half-man/half-donkey laugh that Todd had acclimated to the night before.

"Doesn't matter. Work's work in my book."

Chuck slapped a hand down on his desk. "Good to hear. Not enough people have that attitude these days. Isn't that right, Jolene?"

Jolene nodded while her gaze remained fixed on the world outside the window.

"Like I always say, hard work never killed anyone," Chuck added.

"Unless you work for a bomb disposal unit," Todd tossed in.

It took Chuck a moment before his face lit up and he laughed again, this time, three parts donkey to one part man. Once Chuck had dispensed with the anthropomorphic side of himself, he slid over a map and a stapled sheaf of papers.

"Up for a management job?"

Management job? Todd hadn't expected that. "Yeah, sure."

"Good. You're my new Property Manager."

"Wow."

"Do you hear that, Jolene? The kid's excited."

"He sounds ecstatic," Jolene said, sounding anything but.

"Don't get too excited, Todd. The job sounds impressive, but it isn't," Chuck said with sincerity.

Don't sugarcoat it, Todd thought.

"The job is pretty simple. I maintain a number of rental and unoccupied properties. These need to be checked out on a regular basis to ensure the renters haven't trashed the places and that unoccupied ones haven't been vandalized. Sound good?"

"Sounds good."

"Great. I've highlighted the ones Lyle, J. G., Theo and I own. Take special care with our nest eggs."

Todd flicked through the pages listing the properties owned by Moran and his drinking buddies. If they were nest eggs, then they didn't have much to look forward to in their dotage.

"Will do," Todd said and stood.

Chuck raided the petty cash for a hundred dollars gas and eating money and told him to come back when it ran out. He promised to pay Todd two-fifty a week, cash, with Fridays being payday.

After returning to the pickup and looking up the first address, Todd hit the road. Within a handful of miles, a dark cloud settled on his shoulder. Two-fifty a week. He was in a dead-end job again. Worse still, he had less than he did when he was back in the Bay Area. Sure he possessed six kilos of cocaine and a Lexus, but both were worthless. Making matters worse, he was in deep again. He was supposed to be shedding his old life to start anew, but Vandrel had him over a barrel. All Todd's rebirth money was tied up in this job.

He wasn't totally penniless. He did have the hundred bucks gas money. It wouldn't get him far, but it was enough to cover the price of a bus ticket. He could start afresh somewhere else. Again. Okay, it might mean dead-end jobs for a while but he could get out from under. He wasn't in as deep with Vandrel as he was with the small man. Vandrel had nothing on him. He could get away clean.

He sensed getting away clean would become his mantra. Even if he hadn't been saying it in the past, it was certainly his *modus operandi* in recent years—screw up, run away to start all over again. He guessed he could do that a few more times, but there was only so much road. Eventually, he wouldn't have anywhere to run to.

He'd stick this one out and hope the small man's assessment that he had an aptitude for this kind of work held true.

* * *

The first property Todd came to belonged to Moran. It consisted of a dilapidated farmhouse with a collapsed barn on four acres of desert scrub. A county road gave up on connecting the property to civilization.

What the hell did Moran want with a piece of crap like this? Todd wondered. Moran had probably bought it for a song, but it was hardly a song worth singing. He bounced over the dirt drive to the farmhouse, parked and inspected the "nest egg."

Todd walked the perimeter of the farmhouse. He was no building inspector, but this place was a tear down. The siding curled away from the frame. Shingles dotted the ground where they'd fallen off the roof. The house possessed a slight list that screamed imminent structural failure. He would have liked to have checked out the interior, but couldn't courtesy of some pretty impressive padlocks. Even the windows had been nailed shut.

He had no idea why Chuck had wasted his time sending him out here to check on the place. You'd have to be a pretty desperate vandal to come out here and trash this crap. He didn't see any point in noting down the condition of the property for Chuck unless the place fell down. He had reached the pickup when he noticed a set of well-defined tire tracks leading to the barn.

Maybe there was good reason to have this place inspected on a regular basis. He retrieved the .357 from the glove box, glad he'd brought it along with him, and followed the tracks to the broken-down barn.

He aimed the .357 inside the crooked doorway and peered inside. Light penetrated the gaps between the wood planks to give him a reasonable view of the interior. He ventured inside. Nothing of interest presented itself. The tire tracks went only as far as the entrance. Not that that was a surprise. The structure creaked every time the wind blew. He knelt and scooped up a handful of straw from the thin layer scattered on the ground and brought it to his nose. It was fresh.

"Who's been coming out here?"

His curiosity was getting the better of him, but it would have to wait. There were other Moran properties to inspect. He wondered if he'd find more of the same. He dropped the straw and returned to his pickup.

The distance between properties was vast and he didn't make it out to all of them. He managed to check out one of Chuck's properties, two of J. G.'s and two of Moran's. In most cases, the properties were of the same ilk as the first—large parcels of land in the middle of nowhere. One of Moran's holdings proved to be a true rental though. He logged the renters' complaints of a rundown six-unit complex about a mile from the Texan. Instead of driving back into Dumont to drink away the night at The Yellow Rose, he drove to Vandrel's. He found the old man there, but not the Lexus.

"Where's my car?" Todd asked, entering the hangar.

Vandrel had his feet up on a desk in a small space that passed for an office, listening to his country western spilling from a radio perched on a shelf. He turned the radio's volume down. "Your car? I distinctly remember you saying it was stolen."

Todd saw this was going to be one of those conversations. "Okay, the car I brought you. Where is it?"

"Gone. Sold. Got good money for it too. Better than I expected. I guess Jap cars are popular."

Todd leaned against the desk next to Vandrel's dust-encrusted work boots. "Do I get any of it?"

"That weren't the deal, son. You get paid when you bring me the contents of Moran's safe."

Todd said nothing.

"How's it going with the son of a bitch?" Vandrel asked.

"It's going."

"That bad, huh?"

"Not as bad as you think."

Vandrel smirked.

Todd wasn't going to allow himself to be drawn into an argument and tried a different tack. "I'm assuming you know Moran well."

Vandrel nodded.

"Why would he buy up undeveloped parcels of land with rundown shacks on them?"

Vandrel took his feet off the desk and straightened in his seat. "He wouldn't. He doesn't spend a penny until he knows he's getting a dollar back. What have you found out?"

Todd told him. When he finished, he asked, "Mean anything to you?"

Vandrel shook his head. "Keep digging, son. I think you could be on to something."

"I might need something other than the pickup. Have you got anything else I can use?"

Vandrel tossed Todd the keys to a late model Buick Century and an aging Cadillac Seville. "I don't need to move them any time soon. They run good. What are you thinking?"

"I don't know yet."

* * *

The next morning, Todd went out to the remaining properties on Chuck's list. At the rentals, he took down complaints. One guy tried to mix it up when Todd mentioned that he'd have to pay for a busted bathroom window. Todd escaped in the pickup as the guy retrieved his baseball bat. From then on, Todd kept the .357 on him. The money pit properties owned by Moran and his cronies were more of the same, except in one case. Chuck owned ten acres of dirt on the edge of Dumont. A scorch mark marked the spot where a ranch house once claimed to exist. An explosion looked to be responsible. Debris lay strewn for a hundred feet or so and it all smelled like burnt matches. The foundations were a tattered mess. This seemed to have happened pretty recently.

Todd drove back to Chuck's to report in. He wasn't there and Jolene directed him to the Yellow Rose. Chuck was in his usual spot with his usual friends.

"There's our boy," Moran announced. "We missed you last night."

"I'm a working man now. Early to bed and all that."

"How did it go?" Chuck asked.

"It went okay. I do have bad news. The Parker place, it's been destroyed."

"Oh, that's okay." Chuck ordered a beer for Todd. "I should have told you that before you went out there. Lost the place about a month ago. Damn propane tank took the place out."

Todd was no fire investigator, but he knew Chuck was lying. The explosion had obviously originated from inside the house and it had blasted the propane tank from its mounts. The propane tank was still intact.

"I was going to demo the place anyway. The fire saved me the job," Chuck said and laughed. "Other than that, all good?"

Todd handed over the paperwork Chuck had given him. "I've made notes for you."

Chuck leafed through it. "You've done a nice job. Take the rest of the day off and I'll give you some new addresses tomorrow. You've done well."

"I know a hard working guy when I see one," Moran said and patted the stool next to him.

Todd sat and reached for the beer in front of him. It tasted good after a day cooped up in the pickup with no air-conditioning. He didn't put the beer down until it was half empty.

"How you liking the job?" Moran asked.

"Fine. It's simple work."

"Nobody likes complications."

"Amen to that." Todd raised his bottle and Moran clinked his bottle with Todd.

"You look worried, son."

"No, it's nothing."

"Don't give me that, Todd. We're all friends here."

"Yeah," Chuck said and J.G. slapped Todd on the back.

"Okay. I'm grateful for the job and all, but . . ." Todd hesitated.

"But?" Moran urged.

"It's just that I feel I'm taking your money. I mean, most of the properties I've been out to don't need me checking up on them."

"I know they aren't much to look at," Moran said, "but they're ours and it means a lot to us. It's natural for us to have someone keep an eye on them."

"I guess," Todd said. He wondered if he was playing this hand a little too hard, but didn't think so. He could afford to push a little more. "But why all the rundown properties?"

"Investments," Chuck said.

"They mightn't look it," J.G. said, "but give it time and every one of those properties will make us rich. Ain't that right, boys?"

The boys harrumphed—except for Moran. He'd turned on the snake eyes again. Todd dialed it back and let the subject drop. He needed to get off Moran's radar and announced he needed something to eat, since he hadn't eaten anything all day. Before he could slip out, Theo said dinner sounded good. Chuck seconded him. They left the bar telling Grady not to give up their seats.

Chuck led the way to the Buckeye, a steak house two blocks up from the Yellow Rose. While Moran's boys laughed and joked, Moran just brooded with a storm front for an expression. Todd cursed his stupidity. He'd pushed it too much and Moran was suspicious. He'd have to move things up now.

They ate and Moran added to Todd's discomfort by picking up the tab for everyone. *Nothing like being made to feel like a Judas,* Todd thought.

After the meal, Todd blew off the idea of going back to the Yellow Rose. Moran's boys bitched and whined at him to share a barstool. Todd insisted he couldn't.

"Why?" Moran asked. He put an edge on the question that gave Todd the feeling he was asking more than one question.

"I need an early night is all. I promise tomorrow that I'll make it a late one."

"Whatever you say, tenderfoot," Theo said.

They ribbed him some more, but they let him go. Todd returned to the pickup and drove back to Vandrel's. He exchanged the pickup for the Seville and drove out to Chuck's burnt out property.

He lit up the site with the Caddy's high beams and approached the scorch mark that had once been a house. The stench of charred matches still radiated off the remains as fresh as if the fire had been yesterday and not weeks ago. He kicked over the remains, but unable to connect the dots, he drove off. Maybe Moran's property with the mysterious tire tracks and nailed shut windows might yield more.

During the drive, he wondered if he was making a big mistake. What did the burnt matches smell have to do with anything? And what did he expect to find at Moran's place? Squatters? It could mean something or nothing. It certainly wasn't getting what Vandrel asked him to get. Well, if he turned up nothing but squatters at the other property then he'd do as Vandrel had asked.

As soon as Todd spotted light leaking from the windows of the house, he doused his headlights and stopped the Seville. He left the car on the dirt road and approached the house on foot.

An Econoline van sat parked in the dilapidated barn. No other vehicles were in the vicinity. Todd went up to the van. It was unlocked and the key was in the ignition. Obviously, the unofficial tenants had no fears about security. He touched the van's hood. It was lukewarm.

Music penetrated the house's walls and made it easy for Todd to creep up on the house without being heard. The drapes, essentially sheets nailed up inside, not only failed to keep the light out, but failed to keep him from looking in. He peered through the tears in the thin material into the living room. Two men and a woman, all wearing bandanas, worked furiously around a crudely constructed bench covered with glassware and containers. Todd made out the writing on one container: anhydrous ammonia. Bulk size containers of paint thinner sat next to the ammonia. On the floor, there were enough broken open cold medicine packages to cure a hospital wing of the sniffles.

It was time to go.

* * *

"A meth lab," Vandrel said after Todd had filled him in on the night's discovery.

"I didn't see all the chemicals but that's what it looked like and it explains the burnt out house. Not only are meth guys unstable so is the manufacturing procedure."

Todd peeled back a length of masking tape around the window frame of a Mercedes S-class and tore off the plastic sheeting protecting the window from its new paint job. Vandrel inspected the paintwork for imperfections.

"Okay, someone is setting up meth labs in Moran's abandoned properties. So what are you saying—Moran is a meth producer? Because I don't see it."

"Neither do I. I think he's taken being a landlord to a new level. He's taking on tenants who don't mind the cockroaches and mold, as long as they don't get disturbed. He's letting these tweakers do whatever they do for a slice of the action and if anything goes wrong, well, who cares? Someone will replace them."

"And how does this help me?"

"Now you have something on Moran."

"I don't have spit on him. We cry foul and he's gonna say the drug labs are the work of squatters."

Todd sighed. He'd fallen upon the same conclusion on his ride over to Vandrel's chop shop. "What are you saying—we just give up?"

"You can give up if you want, but you won't get your ten grand. No, we need something tangible on Moran."

"Like what?"

"Paperwork." Vandrel handed Todd a VIN plate to affix to the Mercedes. "Moran might not look it, but he's a packrat. He never throws shit away. That's how he got me. If Moran has dealings with anyone, he makes a record of it."

Todd pop-riveted the VIN plate in place. "Even with drug dealers?"

"Even with drug dealers. You need to break into that safe."

Safecracker. Another talent to add to his résumé. He'd hoped to get the combination before this eventuality. What was it with everyone? They all seemed to think he was capable of any crime. He couldn't crack a nut let alone a safe. Then again . . . hadn't he proved that he did have special talents and aptitudes? A week ago he was struggling to pack boxes in the shipping department. Now he was a pretty successful criminal. He'd yet to make any money, but he'd certainly settled into his new career without too many issues. While he'd failed to make an impact on the corporate world, he'd showed he had the smarts for this dubious career change. If Vandrel wanted a safe cracked then he was the man to crack it.

"When do you suggest I do this?" he asked.

"If you're right and Moran is on to you, like you say, then there's no time like the present."

* * *

Todd drove the Buick back into town and parked on the street. He didn't have to worry about being seen. It was after three and the place was a ghost town. He sneaked a peek at the Yellow Rose. Moran and company might have stayed for an after hours game. He couldn't afford to be up to his elbows in safecracking when they staggered back from the bar. Luckily, the bar exhibited no signs of life.

He went to the rear of Moran's hardware store. If Moran did have any secrets he wanted protecting, he didn't invest too much in security. There was no visible sign of an alarm system. The door was a solid core model with a deadbolt. Todd could bust his way in with a crowbar, but he didn't want to leave a mess. He liked the look of the restroom window. It was small, but not so small that he couldn't squeeze his way through. He stripped off his sweatshirt, pressed it against the opaque glass and smashed the crowbar over the window. The glass splintered after the first blow, but the sweatshirt muffled the earsplitting crack. He brought the crowbar down for a second time and the window fell away. He cleared the glass from the frame, climbed up and clambered through.

Moran didn't have an office. The area behind the counter and cash register was as close as it got. Todd found the safe against the back wall. It wasn't much. To Todd, it looked to be next model up from what hotels used. It was pedestal mounted with four bolts securing it to the floor. If worst came to worst, he could simply unbolt the thing, take it with him and crack it open with a cutting torch back at Vandrel's. But he didn't want to go that route if he didn't have to. He didn't want to keep taking the sledgehammer approach to his newfound career. Okay, busting the window wasn't a good start, but he could work on that. He would pick up a set of skeleton keys and practice on locks. Reading up on safecracking would be another task. He sat down in front of the safe.

He wished he knew Moran better. If he did, it might clue him into a likely combination. He spun the dial to the combination lock hoping to sense the tumbler falling into place. Sadly, he didn't. It was looking more likely that he'd have to unbolt the safe and take it with him, but that was the great thing about ripping off a hardware store. The place was full of tools.

He picked out a power drill and armed it with a half inch bit. He plugged it in and positioned the drill just to the left of the dial. He was about to squeeze the trigger when he heard the unmistakable snap-snap of a pair of hammers going back on a double-barreled shotgun.

"I'd prefer you didn't ruin the safe like you ruined the crapper window," Moran said.

The blood in Todd's veins turned to ice, freezing his body rigid. The .357 was still in the pickup's glove box at Vandrel's. Even if he had it with him, it might as well be at the North Pole for all the good it would do him. Moran had the drop on him.

"You really should clear a building before getting down to business."

"I'm sorry." Todd wanted to say, "it's not what you think," but it was. There was no ducking what he was doing.

"The combination is ten, twenty-seven, sixty-seven," Moran said. "That's my son's birthday, if you're wondering."

Todd raised his hands slowly and carefully above his head.

"You can't open the safe with your hands above your head."

"You want me to open it?"

"You want to see inside, don't you?"

Not really. Not anymore. But Todd did as he was told and fed the combination into the safe. He put his hand on the lever and wondered if this would be his last action on earth. Moran could claim he was stopping a thief with the safe broken open. Todd pressed down on the lever and opened the door.

No buckshot tore him to shreds.

"Remove the contents," Moran ordered.

Todd removed a number of sealed manila envelopes and a small amount of cash.

"See what you're looking for?"

"I don't know."

"Well, take your time. Give everything a good look over before you decide."

"I'm sorry I betrayed you."

"You never betrayed me. It takes a friend to betray someone and you, son, are no friend."

The insult cut deep. In truth, Moran was no friend of Todd's either, but the jibe made him feel inches high.

"The best way to get to know a stranger," Moran said, "is to welcome the stranger. You can't get to know them if you keep them at arm's length." Moran came around the counter with the shotgun barrel and got himself close enough that he couldn't miss. "You're not too smart, are you, son?"

"It doesn't look that way."

"No, it doesn't. This is a small town with only one motel and you weren't checked into it."

"I could have been bedding down in my pickup."

"Yeah, you could have been, but no one saw your pickup parked on the streets and if you were, the moment you were offered a job, a sensible man would have asked for a room or a handout, but you didn't."

Moran was handing Todd his ass in a hat, but at the same time, he was giving him an invaluable lesson. He was new at this game and he would make a few mistakes along the way, but he wouldn't make the same mistake twice. That was if he ever got out of this one.

"You're not a cop, Todd, are you?"

"No."

"Is Todd your real name?"

"Yes."

"Good. I'm glad you didn't lie about everything. You aren't an opportunist, so who are you working for?"

"Me," Vandrel answered, emerging from the restroom with a 9mm in his hand.

Moran swung the shotgun in Vandrel's direction and Todd felt the sweat dry on his back.

"After all these years, you finally got off your ass."

"Is it there?" Vandrel asked Todd.

Todd shone his flashlight on the sealed envelopes. Nothing was marked "incriminating evidence on Vandrel" or "meth labs." All the envelopes were seemingly for monthly invoices. He ripped the envelopes open and poured out the contents. Invoices. Nothing but invoices.

"There's nothing here," he said.

"What?" Vandrel said.

Moran laughed. "What did you expect? That I'd lock everything up in a pissant lockbox? I ain't a fool, Vandrel. You know that."

"Then where is it?" Vandrel demanded, taking two steps forward, his grip tightening on the pistol.

Todd didn't like this. Something was brewing. These guys' feud had been simmering for God only knew how long and he was caught in the crossfire.

"I have a safety deposit box in San Antonio. Everything I've gathered over the years is there. There are a lot of skeletons gathering dust there. Yours included, Vandrel."

"And I've got one of yours," Vandrel answered. "We know all about your little meth lab sideline. Isn't that right, Todd?"

Thanks, Todd thought, *just put me back in the firing line.*

"Is that right?" Moran said, swinging the gun back in Todd's direction.

"You're buying shitty properties out in the middle of nowhere to rent out to scum to make meth," Todd said. "Judging by the scorch mark and the stink, one crew barbecued themselves. But hey, it doesn't matter. There are plenty of tweakers looking for a new place to set up. It's pretty good business too. It's getting harder to set up mobile labs these days especially in the cities so why not come out to big open nowhere where there are no cops and no snoopers to worry about?"

Todd hadn't intended to spill so much. He put it down to nerves. He doubted anyone else had expected the speech either. It was a long time before anyone spoke again.

"You're right. There aren't any snoopers—except for you."

"Don't take it out on him, Lyle," Vandrel said. "He was doing a job for me. If you need to blame anyone, it's me, but you've been blaming me for years."

Moran swung the shotgun away from Todd and aimed it squarely at Vandrel's gut. Todd sensed a violent change in Moran's demeanor. A deep-seated rage melted away his cool. One wrong word and he'd open up with the shotgun.

"You don't know much about our friend here, do you, Todd?" Moran's teasing question squeezed out through gritted teeth.

Todd said nothing.

"Vandrel likes to use people. Young people. Get them to do his dirty work and hang them out to dry when it turns to shit."

"That's not true. What happened to Jesse was an accident."

"My boy died stealing cars for you," Moran bellowed.

"I made a mistake, Lyle. I was fed bad information on the owner. You know how much Jesse meant to me. I loved him like a son."

"But you weren't his father. You don't know a father's pain."

"Then how can you help these killers make their poison? How many other fathers have lost their sons and daughters because of it?"

Todd had to defuse this situation. Guns were going to be used tonight. Whatever information Vandrel hoped to get back, it wasn't going to happen. That left only one alternative—gunplay.

"How do we get to your safety deposit box in San Antonio?" Todd asked.

"You don't," Moran replied.

"We can if you come with us."

"I know what Vandrel wants and he ain't getting it. Do you understand me?"

Moran wasn't talking to Todd anymore. Vandrel answered that he understood.

"Todd," Vandrel said. "I think you should leave now."

"I think that would be a good idea," Moran said.

"Hey, it doesn't have to end this way. It's not over."

"It was over a long time ago," Moran said.

"Todd, if you go back to my shop, you'll find the money I owe you and you can take your pick of the cars," Vandrel said, his tone clipped and abrupt as if his words were holding back a breaking dam.

"Vandrel," Todd insisted.

Vandrel turned his automatic on Todd. "Do as you're damn well told."

Moran stepped back from the counter, unlocked the main door and pushed it open for Todd. Todd didn't have to be asked twice. He squeezed by Moran. In the doorway, he stopped. Moran and Vandrel had turned their guns on each other.

"I'm sorry I let you down, Vandrel."

"You didn't. We're finally going to get this problem resolved."

Moran closed the door.

Todd raced back to the Buick and gunned the engine. He pulled a U-turn to get back to Vandrel's. As he headed out of town, he passed by Moran's hardware store. As the store receded into the distance, two flashes of light from inside it reflected in his rearview mirror.

He didn't stop to check that everyone was okay. It was too late for that. There was only one thing to do now.

Get out of town.

PART THREE
TRADING UP

Todd rode the Greyhound into Dallas. This hadn't been the plan. He'd collected the ten grand from Vandrel's warehouse and hit the road in the Buick. He was going anywhere except Dumont. He was about fifty miles out from town when good sense sank in. Moran and Vandrel had taught Todd a lot about his new life. One thing he'd learned was never to go anywhere without a gun. Everyone needed insurance. He was swapping carriers from State Farm to Smith and Wesson. He might never have to use his insurance, but it was good to have it with him. The second and more important thing he'd learned was a grudge was a grudge was a grudge.

The small man had gone to a lot of trouble to bury Todd, because Todd had screwed up his operations. He'd cost the small man money, personnel and credibility and he wasn't about to forget that in a hurry. It didn't matter where Todd went or what he did to cover his tracks. He was sure the small man would find him and get his pound of flesh.

Todd couldn't risk driving the Buick to Dallas. The car was hot and it would be even hotter when Moran's first customer found the bodies. He couldn't afford to leave a trail all the way to Dallas. He dumped the Buick in Amarillo and caught the bus.

The Greyhound got in early. Over breakfast at a diner, Todd skimmed the yellow pages for Ruskin's dealership. His breakfast partner at the counter remarked he wouldn't go to Ruskin's if he had the choice. Todd had no intention of buying a car from Ruskin's, but he did need wheels. He asked his breakfast partner where he would go to buy a car if he had to choose. He recommended a dealership out towards Rochester Park.

After breakfast, Todd phoned for a cab to take him out there. He picked up a ten year old Toyota Corolla from a nearby lot for three grand. It wasn't much to look at, but the engine was sound. It would do and it still left him seven grand in his pocket. Ready for action, he drove out to Ruskin's.

Ruskin's wasn't a franchise dealership catering to one of the big name car manufacturers. Instead, it was a secondhand dealership catering to the prestige market. Their cars were lightly used. Mercedes and BMWs took up most of the inventory. A fully loaded Infiniti claimed the bottom rung of the "For Sale" ladder.

Todd parked on a side street, slipped out of his jeans and tee shirt and pulled on a pair of dress slacks and a button-down shirt. If he was going to pretend to be a prospective buyer then he had to look like one. He crossed the street and entered the lot. He cast an eye over a Mercedes C-class and wondered if the Lexus he'd been bringing here would have ended up on this lot. It seemed likely.

It took just under a minute before a salesperson smelled blood in the water and zeroed in for the kill.

"Hi," the young, clean-cut woman in her early thirties said. "I noticed you admiring that C-class."

"It certainly looks like my kind of car," Todd remarked.

She presented Todd with her card and introduced herself. "Charlie Ruskin."

Todd fought to keep his surprise in check. Charlie Ruskin was the small man's contact. He'd never said it was a woman.

"So this is your dealership?" Todd asked.

"Sadly, no. It's my father's, but it'll be mine some day. Would you like a test drive?"

"I thought you'd never ask."

She was slick. Todd had to give her that. Instead of running back into the office to grab the keys off the board, she produced them from her pocket and handed them to him.

They got in the car and Todd guided the Mercedes onto the

street. Charlie outlined a route she wanted him to take. It took several minutes to thread the vehicle through the choked streets onto the freeway. This provided Charlie the perfect opportunity to wax lyrical about the qualities of German engineering and craftsmanship. She slipped price into the conversation, which was a bitter pill to swallow, but she sweetened the taste by mentioning the C-class' great resale value. On the freeway, Todd whisked the C-class up to eighty-five without feeling a thing. It drove how a Mercedes should drive.

"How does it grab you?" she asked.

"By the balls and doesn't let go."

"So I can take from that statement that you're interested."

"Very much so. The price is in my range."

She beamed. "We have a deal then?"

"We have a deal."

"How will you be paying?"

"Cash."

"We don't get many of your kind in these parts nowadays."

"Well, I had intended on trading in my previous car, but I had to sell it. Sadly, for well below its blue book value."

"If you haven't finalized the sale and it's our kind of automobile, I'm sure I can make you a better offer. What's the model?"

"A black Lexus with six kilos of cocaine stitched into the back seat and a corpse in the trunk. Interested?"

The color drained from her face, washing away that car-savvy saleswoman persona to reveal a frightened little girl, lost and alone. Todd piled on the pain by producing the .357. He didn't aim it at her. He just let her know that he wasn't going to be a pushover.

"I didn't have anything to do with it. You have to understand that."

"We need somewhere where we can talk."

Charlie directed Todd to Sargent Park. It was small and pleasant, even though a railroad ran through it. They stayed in the car, since Todd didn't want to be overheard. Charlie called into the dealership, told them the sale was a done deal and that she was showing Todd around since he was new to the city. Charlie carried off the lie with conviction. She hung up and clipped the cell phone to her belt.

"What do you want?" she asked.

"To know how it all works."

"Simple really." Her eyes were on the gun. "I receive a call. They tell me a car is coming. When it arrives, I call a number."

"What kind of number? Local? Out of state?"

"Local."

"And what happens when you make the call?"

"We make an arrangement to meet. My contact comes, removes whatever is being transported and goes."

"Who is he?"

"He calls himself Fox, but I don't think that's his name."

"What happens to the car?"

"We dress it up and sell it. That's it. Can I go now?"

"No."

She went to protest, but he tightened his grip on the .357 and she settled down. He felt like a shit for threatening her this way. It wasn't her fault. She was just a cog in the machinery, just like him.

"How did you get mixed up in all this?" Todd asked.

She sagged, seeming to relax, even with the loaded gun pointed at her. "My father. He's a good man, but he's not without his faults."

"What are his faults?"

"There's only one, really. He's a gambler. He'll bet on anything—horses, football, baseball. You name it, he'll put money on it."

"Obviously, he's not a successful gambler."

She snorted derisively. "No. For every dollar he wins, he loses a hundred."

Todd saw where this sob story was heading. "Losses like that mount up."

"Is two hundred and fifty grand a big enough mound?"

Todd said nothing.

She went on to describe how her father's addiction had almost cost them everything. Creditors clued her in to the problem first. They claimed delinquency on bills she swore were paid. When she looked into the accounts, it was all too obvious that her father had been siphoning the sales from the dealership to feed the track and bookies. Before she had a chance to confront him, the money problems went away and a new one started. She received her first phone call telling her to expect an out of state delivery. Her father explained these were the terms of the loan he had with his new lender.

"How long has this been going on?" Todd asked.

"Over two years."

"How often do the calls come?"

"Once a month. Sometimes twice. Last November, it was every week."

"Always drugs?"

She sighed. "I try not to look, but yes. Cocaine."

"All part of a flexible payment scheme. How long before your father's debt is paid off?"

"Will there ever be a final payment?" she said bitterly.

That was the great thing about loan sharks. With interest rates in the stratosphere, there was never any prospect of paying off the principle. The small man had a nice little thing working for him.

"Where's your father now?"

"Retired." The word twisted her features like it had left a sour taste on her tongue. "When the call came to me and not him, he went to pieces. He was no good on the lot. It was for the best."

"Does he still gamble?"

"No. He doesn't go out much and the bookies know not to take his calls." She straightened, regaining her composure after this confessional. "How do you fit into all this?"

"Similar story to you."

Charlie didn't look content to leave it there—gun or no gun—so Todd told her the whole sorry tale. He shouldn't have told her. In a clinch, she could use it against him, but what harm could it do him? None of this was news to the small man. Deep down, he wanted to tell someone. This wasn't something he could share with his closest friend, but he could share it with someone who'd been down the same road. He felt liberated after he told her, but it didn't last long.

"I don't know who your small man is, but my orders don't come from the Bay Area."

"What?"

"My calls come from Seattle."

Todd drove Charlie back to the dealership in silence. They both had plenty on their minds. At the car lot, he got out of the car and handed her the keys.

"I suppose you're not really buying the car," she said.

"Sorry. No."

She shrugged. "It's not the end of the world. I'll tell them you had a change of heart."

"I'd prefer if you didn't."

"And why would I want to do that?"

"Call it a favor."

"A favor for a man who pulls a gun on me? You're asking a lot."

"I know." From the corner of his eye, Todd noticed Charlie's salesmen watching them. "Tell them I'm moving into town and I'll be back in a few days to collect the car." He nodded in the direction of the gawking salesmen.

"And is there a reason for all this?"

"How would you like to pay off your father's debt once and for all?"

* * *

Todd was risking a lot by trusting Charlie Ruskin, but she was in a bind, just like he was. She had to know that the people pulling her strings didn't care about her. If the drug running ever came crashing down on her head, the puppet masters would find themselves another puppet. It was in her best interests to work with him. He'd outlined a plan to her that could set her free. It wasn't without risk, but it could work. Still, she could sell him out. It might buy her a few brownie points with the people in Seattle. That was why he spent the next couple of hours watching Charlie from across the street. She didn't jump on her cell phone the moment he stepped off the lot and no one unusual visited her. She looked to be playing it his way.

He returned to his Toyota and went in search of a motel. He found a place that wouldn't keep his details on file and didn't object to cash. He looked forward to the day he didn't have to hide out in crappy accommodations to avoid someone tracking him down and putting a bullet in him.

He changed out of his formal clothes into jeans and a tee shirt. Thoughts of Seattle crept to the forefront of his mind. If the scheme to use stolen cars to traffic drugs originated in Seattle, then what was the small man's part in it? Was this a side business or his role in someone else's empire? Todd liked to think it was the latter. If the small man was a small fish, then he had to report to someone bigger. The bigger boss would have the power to squash him. But if he was the head honcho, then there was no hope of toppling him.

Too nervous to eat, Todd drove back to Ruskin's Dealership. By the time he reached the car lot, everyone had left for the day, except Charlie. He parked on a side street. He didn't want the Toyota to tip anyone off. He walked into Charlie's office just as the sun deserted Texas in favor of California. She looked how he felt.

"Still want to do this?" Todd asked.

"No, but I'm going to anyway."

He smiled. "Join the club."

He coached her on what to say then made her repeat it to him three times. He wanted to go for a fourth but she lost her temper, complaining she wasn't a damn actress. It was a fair point. If she rehearsed too hard, her performance would come over as just that—a performance.

"Okay, then," Todd handed Charlie the phone, "let's get this party started."

Todd sat close so that he could listen in. His cheek brushed against hers. Her skin felt good against his. He smelled her perfume. It had faded during the day, but it accented her natural scent. He smelled alcohol too. He didn't blame her. He could do with a drink himself.

She punched in the number to her local contact, and when he answered, she said, "It's Charlie. We've got a delivery."

"A delivery?" Fox said. "We're not expecting a delivery."

"I know, but he's here."

"I'll check it out and call you back."

"No." Charlie put just the right note of fear in the word. "Come now. Please."

That stopped him in his tracks. "Why? What's wrong?"

"It's the guy. He scares me. He's—" she groped for a word.

"He's what?" Fox encouraged with a note of anger building in his voice. It wasn't directed at Charlie but at the non-existent courier. It seemed that Fox liked Charlie, which might play to their advantage. "Tell me, Charlie."

"He seems violent. He's not the usual driver we get. There's something wrong about him. He means trouble."

"What car does he have?"

"A black Lexus."

"Keep him there. I'll be there in thirty."

"Hurry," she begged and hung up.

"Wow, you're good," Todd said.

She smiled. "I have my moments." Then the smile fell away. "Usually when I'm scared."

Todd wanted to tell her not to be, but couldn't. He was just as scared. He had no feel for the person on his way over to them. The guy might be a pushover when it came down to it, but that was wishful thinking. It was more than likely this guy was going to be all fireworks. Todd had the bad feeling he'd have to use the gun the small man had planted on him.

Charlie led Todd to the service bays where the exchanges took place. Todd wanted everything to go down here. Fox would be edgy because he was expecting a hostile situation with Todd, the little drug mule that could, but he would be comfortable in these surroundings. He'd feel that he knew the location and think he had the upper hand. Well, he wouldn't be expecting the welcome wagon Todd had in store for him.

The service shop was clean and free of oil stains. If it hadn't been for the telltale odor of engine oil and other lubricants, Todd would have believed the place was never used. That was to be expected with a prestige automobile dealership, he supposed. Clients expected clean, modern and efficient. He was more used to jalopy shops where the oil was so saturated into the floors Exxon could drill to reclaim it.

"Which door will he come to?" he asked.

"That one," Charlie replied and pointed at the main rollup door.

"Good." He rolled a pair of tool chests over to the door and positioned them to the right of the entrance to create a blind spot. He hid behind the chests.

"What should I do?" Charlie asked.

"Do as I told you. I just need you to distract him and I'll take it from there. Just be ready to react if and when things get messy."

Messy. Could things go any other way? Probably not. Todd

removed the .357 from the back of his waistband and checked that all the rounds were safe and snug in their chambers. The backsides of six cartridges stared back at him, just like they had all the times before. It wasn't like they were going to fall out or mutiny against him, but he still checked and double-checked and triple-checked—and give it a minute, and he'd probably quadruple-check. He took comfort in the OCD tendency he'd developed. It helped pass the time.

"Do you think he'll come alone?" Charlie asked.

Todd never considered the connection arriving with his crew. That changed everything. His plan wouldn't work. He couldn't take on a crew alone. He emerged from behind the tool chests. "I thought he worked alone."

"He does."

"Then what makes you think that he'll bring friends along now?"

"Wouldn't you?"

Given the choice, Todd would. "It's a bit late now. We're gonna have play this as it comes."

"Do you think you can handle this?"

"What choice do I have?" He returned to his hiding place and checked the chambers for shells again.

* * *

A fist pounded on the rollup door and a gruff voice called Charlie's name. Traffic must have been kind. He was five minutes early according to Todd's watch. The fist pounded on the door a second time. The door shook on its track and sounded like thunder. Todd eased the hammer back on the .357.

Charlie's spiked heels clicked on the concrete floor. He peered through the gap between the tool chests and watched her approach the door. She pressed a button and the door retracted. Before it had a chance to open fully, Fox ducked under it. He was tall, easily six-feet, and in his early forties with an athletic build. None of that bothered Todd. The guy's smell did. Fox reeked of crime. Todd saw it in the way he entered the shop and systematically scanned the room. He moved with a predator's pace. Oh yeah, this guy was obviously a career criminal. He drove the point home with the automatic he held.

"Where is he?" Fox growled.

"He's not here," Charlie said and pressed the button to close the door.

"You said he was."

Fox stopped in the middle of the shop. He was facing in Todd's direction, cutting off any chance of a surprise attack.

"Turn him around, Charlie," Todd murmured under his breath.

"I know, but after I hung up, he said he wanted something to eat."

Fox cursed. "Where's the Lexus?"

"He drove off in it."

Fox cursed again.

"He should be back in a minute." Charlie circled Fox, which forced him to turn his back towards Todd.

"Good girl," Todd murmured.

"That gives us time to prepare," Fox said.

"Prepare for what?"

"What do you think?" he spat.

Nice. At least I know now, Todd thought. The small man still held his grudge. This wasn't going to end unless he or the small man ended it.

"I can't have you kill him here," Charlie said.

"I don't think you've got a choice, darlin'." Fox tucked the automatic into the back of his jeans.

Todd knew the guy would never be so close to being unarmed again. He charged out from behind the tool chests. "DEA. Hold it right there."

Claiming he was a representative of the DEA was a last second thought. Gun against gun, Todd guessed Fox had more than an edge on him, but that might be canceled out if Fox believed Todd was a government agent. Killing a nobody might not faze him, but killing a federal agent might quell his murderous tendencies.

It didn't.

Fox shot Charlie a venomous look of hatred, then spun around and reached for his weapon. Charlie backed away as Todd closed in on Fox. Every foot closer Todd got to Fox improved his chances of hitting him.

"Don't even think about it," Todd warned.

Fox ignored Todd and jerked out his weapon.

Todd had him. It would have been so easy to shoot, to put a hole in one of the problems and make it go away, but he couldn't. He needed the guy alive. He needed him to talk. As Fox aimed, Todd dropped his aim and his shoulder, and plowed into the man.

Fox read Todd's move all too well. He stepped outside of Todd's collision course, caught his charging body and hurled him across the floor. Knowing he was going down, Todd grabbed Fox's waistband and brought both of them crashing to the ground. Todd cracked his head on the concrete floor and a starburst went off behind his eyes. It dazed him for a second, but only a second. He couldn't afford more than that. Fox was recovering from his fall. Todd tried to tighten his grip on the .357, but found he'd lost the gun in the melee.

"You piece of shit," Fox barked and kicked Todd in the stomach. The kick rolled Todd onto his back. Fox stepped on Todd's neck and lazily aimed his automatic at Todd's face. "DEA, my ass."

Todd tried to speak, but Fox pressed down with his foot, turning Todd's words into a gurgle. Starlight filled his vision. He flailed at Fox's pant leg in an attempt to get the man's foot off his throat.

"DEA or no DEA, you don't leave here tonight." Fox trained his weapon on Todd's face. "Pick an eye. Grunt for left. Gurgle for right." He pointed the gun at Todd's left eye, then his right, then back to his left.

A strangled noise Todd hadn't intended made it past his constricted windpipe.

"Was that a gurgle? Sure sounded like it." Fox grinned. "Right eye it is then."

A gunshot roared in the shop, bouncing off the walls and the parked vehicles. A red blossom opened up on Fox's chest. Confusion and pain stained the man's expression. He staggered back, taking his foot off Todd's throat.

Todd sucked in a much-needed breath. Fox wasn't going down and Todd wasn't about to give the son of a bitch a second chance. He snapped to his feet and drove an unforgiving punch into Fox's wound. Fox's scream filled Todd with satisfaction and he followed up his first punch with a right hook to the guy's jaw that sent a crackle of electricity through the bones of his fist and all the way into his shoulder. The legs went out from under Fox and he collapsed in a heap. Todd tore the automatic from Fox's grasp and aimed it at him.

Charlie's heels beat a tattoo on the concrete. She jammed Todd's .357 in Fox's face and pulled back on the trigger. Todd slapped her arm out of the way as the gun went off. The bullet struck the ground, ricocheting off the concrete to embed itself in a wall.

"I need him alive," Todd shouted. He left out that he didn't want to bury a second body.

Charlie looked at him like he'd slapped her. "He would have killed you."

"It's okay. He can't hurt us now." He reached over and took the .357 from her trembling hands.

"That's what you think," Fox laughed.

"Shut it or else," Todd snarled.

"Or what? You just said you couldn't kill me. You're not very good at this."

"I said I needed you alive. I didn't say anything about being nice about it." Todd ground his heel into Fox's wound. Fox squirmed and did his best to keep in a yell that burst out of him in a rush. Todd took some small pleasure from inflicting this pain but not much. He had to put up a front though. This guy had to believe that he was capable of anything. "Charlie, find something to tie this bastard up with."

Charlie returned with a lifting sling. Todd jerked Fox's arms behind him and looped it around his wrists to produce makeshift handcuffs. He hooked the slack on the hook of an overhead winch and hoisted Fox's wrists up behind his back and jerked him forward, but kept it just low enough to keep Fox's feet on the ground. It looked damned uncomfortable, which was just the effect Todd was hoping to achieve. The answers should come quick.

"See that?" Todd spun Fox to face the untidy puddle of blood spoiling the otherwise spotless floor. "You're bleeding bad."

"You ain't no DEA," he said scornfully.

"I don't think it matters what you think." Todd pressed his thumb into Fox's bullet wound. His thumb touched something hard that wasn't bone. His stomach lurched. This was a road he didn't want to venture down, but he had no choice. This was the only language Fox understood. He'd respond to it. Todd had to believe that.

Fox screamed out and Charlie winced and looked away.

"All you need to know is that you're in a no win situation," Todd said.

"And how do you figure that, tough guy?"

"Do I need to hold up a mirror, moron?"

"This is nothing. They'll give me a pat on the back for this."

"They'll put a bullet in the back of your fucking head when they see you."

Fox snorted derisively.

"They won't let you keep on breathing after you compromised their operation."

"Oh yeah?"

Todd reached inside Fox's back pocket, jerked out his wallet and pulled out his driver's license. "Yes, Wade Mears of Plano. They can't afford errors and you can't stop making them."

"That's not me."

"I think it is. It took you less than thirty minutes to get here. How far is Plano from here, Charlie?"

"Less than thirty minutes away."

"Christ, don't you have any brains? You don't bring ID with you."

Mears cursed under his breath.

"Did you let anyone know you were coming here tonight?" Todd asked.

"Worried about the cavalry?"

Todd slammed a fist in Mears' wound. "Did you talk to anyone?"

Mears breathed hard from the punch. "No."

That was good. It meant no loose ends. This could be explained away if no one beyond the three of them knew about this.

The color was draining from Mears' face. Todd guessed it had less to do with his shock and more to do with his blood loss. Mears wasn't losing a lethal amount, but he had to be going lightheaded. Todd had to hurry this up.

"I can crucify you, Wade, but I can save you too."

"Blow me."

Todd thumbed Mears' bullet again with the desired effect. "I demand a little respect, Wade. Especially considering the position you're in right now."

"And what position is that?"

"Fucked." Todd paused to let the enormity sink in. "You're shot and unless you're a premed student, I don't see how you can avoid a hospital and a hospital means cops. I'm sure you have friends, but that means word getting back and that means questions. Questions you'll have a hard time answering. Questions that lead to answers that are punctuated with a bullet." Todd showed Mears his own gun. "I can compound those problems by putting a kilo of uncut coke in your lovely home detailed on this driver's license. No matter how you slice it, someone will come gunning for you."

"You two will have to explain this mess too."

Todd turned to Charlie. "Not really. I could be a bastard and say it's not my problem. This isn't my dealership."

Charlie frowned. Todd smiled.

"But it's not even an issue. Who's going to believe that Charlie runs a drug mule business out of here, Wade?"

Mears didn't answer.

"Yeah, I didn't think so," Todd remarked. "So Wade, what's it to be—the cops, them or me?"

Mears pondered his options. Surprisingly, not as long as Todd imagined.

"What do you want?"

"You mentioned they. Who are they?"

"You think I'm going to tell you that?"

"Don't make me state the obvious again," Todd said impatiently.

"What do I get out of this?"

"Tell me something useful and I might just tell you."

"I work for the Carlsons."

"And where would I find the Carlsons?"

Todd prayed for the answer to be in California, but it wasn't to be. Just like Charlie, Mears' orders came from Seattle. Questions about the small man's role in this scheme filled Todd's head again, but he had no answers to make them go away.

"How about San Francisco—deal with anyone there?"

"No."

"Sure? This is important, Wade."

"Yes."

Todd pressured Mears for more. He pressed at the bullet wound a couple of times just to make sure Mears wasn't holding out, but he knew nothing about the small man. He knew the Carlsons and that was it. He spilled contact numbers, meeting places and names. It surprised Todd that Mears knew that much. At the end of the day, he was a satellite on the outskirts of the organization, just a drone doing their bidding.

When he'd given up all he was going to give, Mears asked, "Can I get some water?"

"Sure," Todd said. "You've earned it."

Charlie filled a paper cup from the cooler and held it to Mears' mouth for him to drink.

"I think he's had enough. Lower him," Charlie said.

She fixed Todd with a disgusted look. Todd nodded and lowered the hoist until Mears rested on his knees. Mears let out a groan of relief.

Before Todd unhooked Mears and cleaned him up, he bound his wrists and ankles with duct tape. Mears seemed docile enough, but Todd wasn't taking any chances. He wouldn't put it past him to fight back. Todd sure as hell would if he were in his bloodied shoes.

After they'd patched Mears as best as they could, Todd washed the blood off him in the restroom. Charlie followed him in. She looked haggard. Her hair hung limp around her face and her sun kissed complexion had bled away to a ghostly white. Todd imagined this whole business had aged her. She would have grown up a lot more than she liked when daddy's gambling problems brought mobsters to her door.

"What are you going to do with him?" she asked.

"Let him run."

"Can we trust him?"

Todd exhaled. "We don't have much of a choice, but I think so. He's got just as much to lose as we have. I'll reinforce the fact when I cut him loose."

Fear filled her expression. He'd seen it several times while he questioned—no, interrogated—Mears. It wasn't time to get squeamish over what he'd done.

"You scared me out there," she said.

Truth be known, he'd scared himself too. He was changing. Some of it for the better and some of it not. "You know the position I'm in. Yours isn't a lot different. Tonight was never about negotiation. I had to get what I wanted without it coming back to bite me."

"And did you get what you wanted?"

"Some. Not enough, but enough to be getting on with."

"Hey," Mears bellowed. "Cut me loose."

Charlie shook her head slowly.

"Sounds like our guest is getting restless," Charlie said.

They returned to their noisy captive, Todd drying his hands on a long ream of paper towel.

"Here come the executioners," Mears taunted. He wriggled slug-like across the floor, and just like a slug, his bloody shoulder left a trail behind him. Todd knocked him onto his back with his foot, ending his escape.

"So you think we're going to kill you?" Charlie asked in a neutral tone.

"Let's not play games. We all know the rules. You're gonna tell me I'm free to go then you're going to put a bullet in the back of my head."

"Wade, I don't have to get my hands dirty with you." Todd dropped to one knee. "When word gets out—and it will, I'll make sure of it—the Carlsons will do the job for me. But I realize you're just a foot soldier doing your job, so I'm going to cut you some slack. You split. Tonight. I'll promise to forget all about you."

"It's the best offer life is ever going to throw you," Charlie added.

Mears looked from Todd to Charlie and back. Skepticism claimed his expression.

"Got any cash?" Todd asked.

"About a grand."

It was more than Todd had on him when he'd skipped out on the small man. "That should get you a long way if you spend it wisely."

Something melted in Mears' expression. "You're serious, aren't you?"

"Do I have to poke you in the shoulder to prove it?" Todd asked.

Mears cracked a smile. "You ain't no DEA agent."

"Does it matter?"

"No."

"We got a deal then?"

"If you cut me loose, we can shake on it."

The fable of the scorpion and the toad flashed through Todd's head. "I'll take your word on it. Got a car?"

"Green Caddy parked on the street. Keys are in my pants."

Todd fished for the keys and tossed them to Charlie. She backed the Cadillac into the garage and helped Todd load Mears into the Cadillac's trunk. They struggled against his buckling and bitching.

"I should have known you'd fucking lie."

Todd pinned Mears' head to the trunk's carpeted interior and looked him directly in the eyes. "Wade, I'm not lying. I'm not going to kill you, but I'm also not just going to let you walk out of here. I'm taking you to neutral ground. Okay?"

"You'd better be."

"Or what, Wade? You aren't in a position to make threats."

Todd slammed the trunk lid down before Mears could bitch further.

"What do we do now?" Charlie asked.

"Know anywhere remote?"

"You're not going to kill him, are you?"

Todd shook his head. "No, I just want to get him out of the way for a while."

She nodded. "I know somewhere."

Charlie led the convoy in her Audi. Todd followed in Mears' Cadillac. They drove out to Bynum. It was quiet, remote and a good hour from the city. They freed Mears from the trunk and perched him on the rear bumper. He looked ghastly. The blood loss was taking its toll.

"Know someone who can take care of the bullet?" Todd asked.

Mears nodded.

"Are they connected to the Carlsons?"

He shook his head.

"Good."

Todd went through the Caddy. He wanted to make damn sure the son of a bitch didn't have a spare weapon or anything that he could use on them. The car was clean.

Todd pulled out Mears' automatic and handed it to Charlie. "Keep that on him."

She did exactly as she was told.

Todd pulled out a box cutter he'd snagged from the workshop and cut the tape around Mears' ankles. "Remember who is giving you this wonderful opportunity to live."

"Some opportunity," Mears grumbled. When he realized that Todd wasn't going to cut the rest of the tape until he got a satisfactory response, he said, "I'll remember you until my dying day. Good enough?"

Todd sliced open the remaining tape. "Move over there."

Mears stood, but tottered. He stopped when he was about twenty feet away from the Cadillac. He wavered for a moment before falling to the ground in a heap.

"Are we all square?" Mears asked.

Todd jammed the box cutter into a tire. "Now, we are."

"You shit."

"Have a good life, Wade. Play it smart and it'll be a long one."

Todd and Charlie returned to her Audi and raced off before Mears got to his feet.

* * *

Charlie's speeding Audi crossed Dallas' city limits and she asked, "Is that story about you and the small man true?"

"Yes."

She pondered Todd's one word answer for far too long.

"Why do you ask?" he asked.

"The way you handled yourself tonight. It didn't seem like the first time you had to get information out of a person."

She was right. Even Todd struggled with it. The Todd he knew couldn't bullshit someone like Mears, let alone torture him. Again, the small man's words rang inside his head. He had an aptitude for this kind of work and he was getting better at it all the time.

"I don't know what to tell you, Charlie. We're capable of anything when we're backed up into a small enough corner. Who would have thought you'd be part of a drug distribution ring?"

It was a cruel thing to say, but it had to be said. Charlie was in no place to play the morality card and more importantly, he didn't want her to view him as a bad guy. Charlie absorbed the barb with good grace and nodded.

They drove in silence for the rest of the journey. She parked her Audi inside the workshop. The place had taken on a different appearance. Even ignoring the blood, it didn't look as clean.

Todd found a mop to clean up the blood, but Charlie stopped him.

"I'll clean up. You need to go."

She was right. Even in his current condition, Mears should have changed the tire by now. Todd's window of escape was shrinking.

Charlie offered him Mears' automatic.

"No, you keep it," he said.

"As a memento?" she joked.

He smiled. "No. For protection. There's going to be some fallout when the Carlsons realize their handler has skipped town."

"Or he tells about tonight," she said.

Todd shook his head. "He knows his days are numbered unless he disappears."

"What do I do when the next car arrives?"

"Hopefully it won't."

"But if it does."

"Play dumb. Tell them that you tried to contact Wade, but he doesn't answer. They'll search for him and probably assign someone else to collect the drugs."

"So nothing's changed."

"It will. Give me time."

Charlie viewed the weapon and her smile evaporated.

"I wish I could stick around to help," he said.

"No. You need to go. Besides, I don't think I could survive another day with you around."

He flushed.

"So, I guess you're off to Seattle to see the Carlsons and get the small man off your back."

"Yes."

"Do you think you'll succeed?"

He shrugged. "You never can tell. I might even get them to consider your loan paid up."

Her smile came back. "That would be nice."

"It would be, wouldn't it?"

She was still smiling when he walked out the door.

PART FOUR
HE SAID, SHE SAID

Todd reached Seattle by Wednesday morning. If he'd pushed it, he could have made it the day before, but he saw no reason to rush. For once, he left a city without a tidal wave of trouble looming over him. This was the time he could afford to take things at his own pace. The small man wasn't going anywhere any time soon and neither were the Carlsons. At last, the tail wasn't wagging the dog.

He rewarded his Toyota with a trip to an oil changers after its two thousand mile drive. Leaving the car in their capable hands, he went in search of a payphone. He called the number Mears had given him.

"Hello," the woman's voice said with exaggerated cool.

"Yeah, my name's Todd and I'm looking for work."

"I'm sorry this isn't an employment agency. You have the wrong number."

"I was told the Carlsons always had work," Todd blurted before she hung up.

"Who told you that?" She had an edge to her voice.

Todd reeled off the story Mears had told him to use. He'd been practicing it on the long drive up from Texas and it sounded convincing, even to his ears. The key that opened the doors to the kingdom of crime involved a guy called Munson. Munson had worked for the Carlsons at one time until a botched larceny got him busted. He'd held his tongue and did the time without ever mentioning the

Carlsons. The Carlsons rewarded him with a retirement home and an allowance in Florida. Now, if he came across a guy he liked, he sent him to Seattle. The beauty of this was that the Carlsons couldn't check with Munson. The cops had never believed he worked alone and they hadn't taken the tail off him. The upshot of this was that the Carlsons never made contact with the man again. The whole thing relied on faith. He hoped Mears hadn't lied about all this. He doubted it. The story was too intricate and too involved for Mears to invent while being tortured.

"So how is Munson?" the woman asked, at last showing signs of warmth.

"Shitty. His busted knee doesn't do well even in Hobe Sound."

Apparently, this detail unlocked the door. He was in. The woman reeled off an address.

"Know where that is?" she asked.

"I'll find it."

Todd bought a mocha and Danish at a Tully's and consumed them on the way back to the oil changers. The manager dealt the bad news that his Toyota wasn't long for this world if he didn't have a whole host of parts replaced. Todd told the manager that the Toyota had been through a lot and it wasn't fair to keep putting it through more. Sometimes you just had to leave things in the hands of God. The manager didn't appreciate the humor and failed to smile when Todd took the keys from him.

Todd bought a map at a local gift shop and drove to the address the woman had given him. The address turned out to be a mixed-use building a couple of blocks from Pioneer Square. Although within spitting distance of the tourist spot, the revitalization failed to stretch this far. The buildings on either side were rundown. The commercial space below the residential was boarded over. He climbed the short flight of steps leading to the door of the residential part of the building and pressed the button to 2A. There was no name attached.

"Yes?" a woman answered.

"It's Todd. We spoke on the phone."

She didn't answer, but the buzzer screeched at him and the door unlocked, so he went in.

The hallway was cold and uninviting from the lack of heating. He climbed the stairway to the second floor and found 2A. The door was ajar. He let himself in.

2A was nothing like the rest of the building. Where everything else was rundown, 2A was plush. Expensive furniture was nestled knee deep in thick carpeting. The lighting was subdued. The temperature was kept at a toasty optimum. Todd felt at home.

Click!

That at home feeling scurried off just as quickly as it had arrived. Someone had pressed a gun to the back of Todd's head. He raised his hands.

"Take it easy," he said.

"Don't tell me what to do," the woman said. "I knew it would come to this."

"Come to what?"

"Don't play dumb."

It was the only thing he could play. Then he cursed himself in his thoughts. Mears had screwed him. The Munson story was just that—a story. Bastard.

She patted him down and found the .357 in the back of his pants. She jerked it out and pressed it against his spine.

"I suppose you carry that for protection, huh?" she asked.

There was no right answer to a question like that, so he kept his mouth shut.

She swiped the .357 across the back of his head. The blinding white light in his vision dropped him to his knees. He put his hands to the point of impact.

"I asked you a question." She planted a kick to his liver that sent him onto his face.

Two hits and he was down. Yeah, he was a real tough guy. When would anything go his way?

"I thought the question was rhetorical," he squeezed out before she assaulted him further.

She laughed. "Rhetorical? An educated idiot. That's a first."

"No, not educated." He rolled over onto his back. "Just a plain idiot."

She laughed again. She might have been laughing, but it was

laughing without humor. Her eye was still on the game. Still on him.

"My question." She pointed a small stainless steel automatic at his face.

"Sometimes I carry the gun for protection."

"And other times?"

"To shoot people."

"At last, an honest answer. Do you want to follow it up with another one?"

"I'll try."

"He sent you, didn't he?"

"Munson? Yes."

She pulled the trigger. The bullet winged past Todd's head and punched a hole in the couch behind him.

"I have a hard time believing Munson sent you when he was killed in a hit and run last month."

Oh Christ, Todd thought. Mears' information wasn't CNN fresh. He was so screwed.

"Do you want to try that Munson story again?" She trained the automatic at his face again.

"Not really."

"Smart man. Why don't you give the truth a little airing this time?"

The truth wasn't an option and Todd hadn't planned on using a backup story, but staring down the barrel of the woman's gun inspired invention. He sold her a story about meeting some drunk in a bar in Missouri who'd told him about the Carlsons. She quizzed him on a description for the drunk. He fed her a nondescript run-down that matched most of the population.

"Sounds like Tucker," she concluded and lowered the automatic.

Todd released a thick breath that hurt his chest and throat on the way out.

"You have no idea who I am, do you?" She sank onto the couch opposite Todd, keeping the gun trained loosely on him.

Todd shook his head, his gaze on her gun hand.

"I'm Jessica Carlson."

Todd felt slapped and he didn't mind its sting. Talk about falling on his feet. He expected he'd have to use some fancy moves to get to the Carlsons. He never thought Mears' information was going to take him right to their door.

"You have no idea how close you came to getting yourself killed," she said.

Todd had a funny feeling he did.

"Did my husband send you?" She snapped her gun arm in his direction. "This time I have no intention of giving you a warning shot. Did he send you?"

"No. I have no idea who he is. Honest. I just came for a job."

"Convince me."

"Look, I don't know what to tell you. I don't know him and I don't know you. I came for a job, not a bullet in the face. Okay?"

She lowered the gun again. What was this? Good Jessica-bad Jessica? Whatever she called this act, it worked. If she didn't let up with this shit, Todd was going to spill the truth.

"You want a job?"

Against his better judgment, he answered that he did.

"When you called me, was I the first person you called about work?"

"Yes."

"You didn't call my husband?"

"No."

"And nobody knows you're in this city?"

"No."

"Then I think I've got a job for you." She stood, gestured to him to follow and led the way to an office area with a desk, a computer and filing cabinets. She reached inside a desk drawer and pulled out a ten thousand dollar bundle of hundreds. She counted out ten bills. "Here's a thousand dollars. Find yourself a room. Somewhere quiet that doesn't ask too many questions. Get bathed. You smell like a goat."

Todd let that one go. There was no arguing the point.

"Then come back and I'll give you another thousand as a down payment."

"For what?"

"For killing my husband."

* * *

The next morning, Todd sat in the passenger seat of his Toyota parked opposite an office building in the financial district. People would pay less attention to him if he were sitting in the passenger seat. If anyone asked what he was doing, he was waiting for a friend. As deceptions went, it was simple yet effective.

Jeff Carlson sat somewhere on the eighth floor of the building. This was the professional face of his business dealings. Unlike the semi-derelict building where Todd had encountered Jessica, the office building was modern. This was the headquarters for Carlson Realty and Carlson Shipping. The building's directory listed software companies, accountancy and law firms, and regional headquarters for a number of Fortune 500 companies. Respectable rubbed shoulders with respectable. Not surprisingly, it was a front. The realty firm helped launder dirty money that the shipping firm generated in the shape of unsavory goods and services. If Jeff's neighbors only knew the truth.

It was a typical Seattle day. Gray with the threat of rain. The weather matched his mood. No wonder so many people committed suicide every year in this place. Guilt was already seeping into him like the dank humidity in the air. He'd agreed to kill this guy. He'd taken Jessica's money, done all the things she'd told him to do and now he was doing the groundwork before pulling the trigger. He thought he'd reached his limit when he'd tortured Mears, but he was wrong. He was way off plan here. Of all the new skills he was learning, killer wasn't one he'd expected to add to his resume. The only way he could justify the killing to himself was the condition he'd applied to Jessica's terms.

"And what's that?" she'd asked.

"I need some information on someone."

"Who?"

"Someone you have business dealings with in San Francisco."

A flicker of recognition shone in her eyes. "When you've completed the job."

It was a fair enough trade, at the time. Now he wished he'd pushed a little harder.

An ex-marine pushed his way out of the building. Todd didn't know for sure if this guy was an ex-marine or not, but he carried himself with that ramrod straightness and a precision that he associated with military. The ex-marine represented half of the double act that lagged behind Jeff Carlson. Todd had to give props to Carlson for that. He wasn't the stereotypical mobster. He didn't draw attention to himself, by surrounding himself with thugs. He drove himself while the jarhead twins followed at a respective distance. Todd took this hands-off approach as a sign of confidence. Jeff Carlson wasn't under the threat of attack. He sat very comfortably in his world. He was his own lord and master. Todd guessed this was also a sign he could handle himself in a clinch. Just his luck.

The ex-marine crossed the street towards the deli on the corner. He placed an order and returned with a large paper sack. *Lunch for the boys*, Todd thought.

Todd's driver's door flew open and a man slid into the seat.

"Hey, what the hell do you think you're doing?" Todd barked.

"Shut the fuck up, before I shoot you." The man, in his forties and blond, jabbed a pocket-sized gun in Todd's ribs.

Todd started to raise his hands, until the blond man told Todd to put them down, remarking, "We're all friends here."

"Friends don't point guns at each other."

"I didn't say we were good friends. Hands in pockets, please." When Todd had stuffed his hands in his pockets, he lifted the .357 from Todd's waistband. "Must be uncomfortable sitting on that."

"You get used to it."

"Jessica hired you, didn't she?"

"Who?"

The blond slammed the butt of his gun down on Todd's thigh, striking a nerve connected to his groin. Todd doubled over and fought the nausea clawing up his throat.

"Don't play games. I might stop liking you if you do. Jessica hired you, didn't she?"

"Yes." Todd's reply came out strangled.

"She wants you to kill Jeff, right?"

"If you know all this, why are you asking?" Todd wondered where he'd gone wrong. Probably from the beginning. He hadn't been looking for anyone because he didn't know he needed to. This was another lesson learnt. Always assume someone is following.

"You don't look like a hitter," the blond said, ignoring Todd's point.

"How do you know? Not all hitters look the same or everyone would spot them."

"How much has she agreed to pay you?"

"Fifteen grand."

The blond laughed. "Yeah, you're no hitter. If you were, you wouldn't touch the job without a zero on the end."

Todd was tired of this twenty questions crap. "Who are you? Bodyguard? Cop?"

"Referee. Guardian angel. A mix of both."

"Thanks for clearing things up for me."

"Hey, enough of the smart mouth." The blond raised his gun up for another hammer blow.

That was enough for Todd to cease and desist.

"You don't know anything about the Carlsons, do you?"

Todd said nothing.

"The Carlsons represent an impressive trading bloc in the Pacific Northwest for all things criminal. And when I say the Carlsons, I mean Jeff and Jessica in equal parts. Jessica is no trophy wife. Their marriage is one of sound business. Two factions ran Seattle. Jeff ran one. Jessica the other. They married for purely financial reasons. Now, Jessica wants to liquidate that arrangement, but she doesn't want to split assets. That's why anyone with an ounce of sense won't touch her hit and why she has to lowball it out to guys like you. No offense."

"And where do you fit into all this as referee and guardian angel?"

"I'm trying to keep them from killing each other."

"Why?"

"Selfish reasons. Seattle is a stable city. Things are under control. If Jessica kills Jeff and assumes control, it will lead to destabilization. Some upstart will think they are entitled and will try to take it from her. I don't want that to happen."

Even organized crime had politicians. *How disappointing*, Todd thought.

"What's your name?" the blond asked.

"Todd Collins."

"I'm Martin Fisk. How would you like to meet Jeff?"

* * *

"Who's this?" Jeff Carlson asked.

"One of Jessica's lost boys," Fisk answered.

Carlson stiffened in his seat. He looked more annoyed than frightened. He tossed a glance the ex-marines' way and they marched out of the office.

Fisk settled into one of the visitor chairs opposite Carlson. Todd did likewise.

As corner offices went, Carlson had a nice one, consisting of the usual modern conveniences required by today's corporate execs. That included the secretary that Todd guessed saw no evil, spoke no evil and heard no evil. She never looked up once from her computer monitor to acknowledge their arrival. The same applied to the dozen or so people working away at their desks. Everyone seemed to be white-collar professionals doing white-collar work. It made for a nice cover. Todd wondered if these people believed they truly worked for a realty and shipping company. It was a reasonable hypothesis, if it weren't for the ex-marines. Their presence spoiled the front. They were a pair of square pegs who did nothing but hang out in an office adjacent to Carlson's.

"My wife hired you to kill me?"

"Yes."

"My wife and I have a complex marriage, Mr. . . . ."

"Todd Collins."

"My wife and I have a complex marriage, Mr. Collins. One that most people wouldn't understand."

"There's no need to explain. It's none of my business."

"Thank you. Correct me if I'm wrong, but you didn't come to Seattle with the sole desire to kill me."

"No. I came looking for work."

"What kind of work?"

Fisk removed Todd's .357 and placed it on the desk. Carlson studied the weapon and nodded like its presence explained everything.

"I'm guessing you aren't a nine-to-five sort of guy?"

"Not anymore."

"Well, I think we can put you to work."

"What do I do about Mrs. Carlson?"

"Tell her she'll have to find someone else," Carlson said matter-of-factly.

Todd thought about her accuracy with a gun and willingness to use one. "And she'll just accept that, will she?"

"Probably not."

"You'll have to do a good job convincing her," Fisk added.

Carlson and Fisk pumped Todd for information. He gave up as much as he could without giving it all up. He was wedged between a pair of hard places after all. They seemed satisfied with his answers. Carlson said Fisk would put him to work starting tomorrow. Fisk handed Todd some walking around money and Carlson handed Todd back his gun. Todd wasn't sure if this was a test of trust or a suicidal bent on Carlson's part. He thought about the four rounds left in the .357's cylinder. Enough for Carlson, Fisk and the ex-marines, but not enough for the witnesses. He slipped the revolver into his waistband.

Back on the street, Todd asked Fisk, "Now what?"

"I've got a lunch date and you've got a parking ticket."

Flapping from the windshield was a newly applied ticket.

"I would pay that. Those things stack up if you don't."

"Thanks."

Fisk produced a cell phone and punched in a number. He told the person answering that he'd be a few minutes late, then hung up.

"Todd, play it square with Jessica. She'll write you off as a pussy that bitched out on her. She'll complain, but she'll move on and find someone else to do the deed."

"What happens then?"

"That's not your problem." Fisk tap-danced down the concrete stairs from the building. "Meet me at Pike Place Market at nine tomorrow. Don't be late."

Todd watched Fisk hail a cab before crossing the street back to his Toyota. He peeled off the parking ticket, screwed it into a ball and tossed it on the backseat. He had no intention of staying in Washington long enough for it to matter.

He returned to the phone booth he'd called Jessica from the day before and called her. "We need to talk," he said.

"I'm busy. Be here at seven, tonight."

He didn't mind the brush off. It gave him time to rehearse his speech.

He returned to the Travelodge where he was staying. It might not be situated in the prettiest part of the city, but it was quiet, clean and a block away from a strip club that boasted hundreds of sexy girls and three ugly ones. It was nice to be amongst honest folks for a while.

He inched by the cramped reception area to get to his room. He made the mistake that women are warned against in parking lots late at night. He didn't have his key handy. He didn't bother to get out his cardkey until he reached his room and that was when they pounced. He didn't even sense them until they drove him face first into the door. The inside of his skull rang with the same off-key tone as the hollow core door when his head bounced off it. Too dazed to fight back, the cardkey was out of his hand and into somebody else's. The door flew open and two sets of hands thrust him into his room then slammed him down onto the carpet. He tried to scream for help, but he only assisted them in inserting a gag into his mouth. Seven seconds later, zip ties bound his hands and ankles behind him and another zip tie bound the ties together to complete the hog tying demonstration. The hands hoisted him up and tossed him onto the bed. Carlson's ex-marines looked down at him, pleased with their work.

Carlson walked into the room and closed the door. He sat on the bed opposite Todd and nodded to one of his thugs. The one Todd had witnessed going out for lunch tugged the gag out of his mouth.

"So my wife hired you to kill me."

"I don't think she's going to take no for an answer."

Carlson laughed. "That sounds like Jessica. Bet you wished you'd been more persuasive."

"Under the circumstances, yes."

"Well, I want to help you out of your difficult situation."

Todd didn't like the sound of that. Handling Jessica was going to be a problem, but not that much of a problem. After Fisk left him, he'd considered getting in his car and just driving off. Sure, he needed information about the small man, but he could find it elsewhere. The Carlsons weren't worth this much crap. But the time to run looked to have just run out.

"How can you help me?" Todd asked, losing sensation in his hands and feet.

"You're going to kill Jessica for me."

"I thought you said—"

"Forget what I said. That was for Fisk's benefit. He's got a thing for Jessica. He thinks he can save her from herself and me. He's wrong. He can't. How does twenty-five grand sound?"

Not that great. Money was being thrust at him from all directions and the numbers kept getting higher every time, but none of it was reaching the echelons Fisk had mentioned.

"Seeing as I know a bit more about the job and the ramifications associated with it, I was thinking of a number in the six-figure range."

Carlson and the ex-marines found that hilarious.

"If you were worth six-figures, I'd pay it," Carlson said, "but you're not. You'll take the twenty-five, which is damn generous for a guy who was planning to put a bullet in me. If you don't, I'll put a bullet in you. Now, what do you think?"

"Twenty-five sounds great."

"Good man." Carlson jerked a nod in the direction of the ex-marines.

One of the jarheads jerked out a switchblade and sliced open the zip ties. The rush of blood back to Todd's extremities forced a sigh of pleasure from him.

Carlson rose to his feet and headed towards the door with his ex-marines in tow. "As far as Fisk knows, this didn't happen," Carlson called out. "Okay?"

Todd didn't move until Carlson was long gone. He rolled onto his back and massaged the red rings around his ankles and wrists. He glanced over at the clock on the nightstand. It wasn't quite two o'clock.

* * *

"It's me" was the magic phrase to open the doors to Jessica's building. She greeted Todd without a gun or a pat down. Music spilled from an unseen sound system. It was low and soothing, but did nothing to take the tension out of the air.

"He's not dead, is he?" she demanded.

"No," Todd replied. "Do you know you're being watched?"

Todd had to keep things tight from now on. He couldn't afford to say too much and risk Jessica's hair-trigger temper. Also, he wanted her opinion of Fisk. Was Fisk the lynchpin in the Carlsons' affairs he believed himself to be?

"Fisk, you mean?"

"Blond guy, mid-forties, stands around five ten."

"That's him."

"Yeah, well, it made it real hard to follow your husband with him tagging along behind me. Who is he?"

Jessica guided Todd to the sofa, sliding in next to him. She laid out a story, which pretty much tallied with Jeff's. Fisk had worked for Jeff since the beginning. She'd noticed him tailing her. At first she'd suspected Jeff just wanted to keep tabs on her, but over time she realized that Fisk had a thing for her.

"That's precious, but that pretty much screws up my chances of killing your husband."

"You've grown some balls since yesterday." She patted his cheek. Condescension shone in her eyes.

"No, I have a sense of urgency. You asked me to kill your husband and that's fine. I can do it—not my thing—but I'll do it. But that's real hard when I've got a witness hanging over my shoulder." Todd's words tumbled out in an avalanche of inspired neurosis. It was a convincing act, because he believed every word. The Carlsons and Fisk were crowding him, cutting off his air. One of them had to give him room.

"Steady there. Don't you worry about Fisk. I'll keep him occupied. Is that all you wanted from me tonight?"

"No. This Fisk knows me. I can't afford to hang around town and to follow your husband until a gap opens up. Your husband is never alone thanks to the two military types that follow behind him at a safe distance."

Jessica smiled. "You've impressed me. I didn't think you'd pick up on them so quickly."

Todd didn't like that remark. What was she expecting? For him to just walk up to him on the steps of his building and cap him there in the street with his bodyguards twenty yards behind? Suddenly, Todd felt the sticky wet stamp of expendable on his back. It made sense from Jessica's point of view. He caps Carlson and the ex-marines cap him. The circle of silence is kept sacred. The money she'd promised him seemed to have shifted from her desk drawer to another hemisphere. Jessica wasn't the one to give him the space he needed.

"So how do you want to play this thing?" she asked.

"I need him alone. I need his entourage to be occupied elsewhere when I do this."

"I think that can be arranged," she said with a cat that's just got the cream look. "Lie low for a couple of days while I sort some things out."

Todd got up to leave.

"I do have one request."

"What's that?"

"I want to be there when you do it."

* * *

Fisk was already waiting at the coffee shop opposite Pike Place Market's north arcade when Todd arrived. Fisk indicated to a waitress for another menu. Todd glanced over the menu but his stomach churned at the thought of food. Nerves were setting in. This was taking too long and getting too messy. He couldn't see himself getting out of this without something sticking to him. The waitress waited for him to order and he disappointed her by just ordering coffee.

"Not hungry?" Fisk asked when the waitress walked off.

"Not much of a breakfast guy."

"You should try. You'll feel better."

Todd sipped his coffee. "Maybe tomorrow."

Fisk's breakfast arrived and Todd's stomach churned at the smell of eggs and sausage. Todd brought his coffee to his mouth so he could distract his nausea with the aroma. Fisk missed the charade.

"What do we do today?" Todd asked.

"We've got a little business over here."

"Doing what?"

"You'll see."

Fisk paid the check and walked Todd to 1st Avenue. He stopped at an Asian-owned knick-knack store at the edge of the market district. It sold the usual touristy crap you found in every big city. A couple of Asian teenagers straightened stock on the shelves and outnumbered the customers. The place smelled freshly decorated. The woman behind the register recognized Fisk immediately and broke into a wail of happy shrieks, not all of it in English. She came out from behind the register to pump Fisk's hand with a two-fisted shake and did the same with Todd. Fisk greeted her in what Todd took to be Chinese. It came out smooth yet practiced.

"Friend?" the woman asked, looking at Todd.

"A colleague, Mrs. Ho. I'm showing him the ropes."

"Good. Good."

Mrs. Ho called over the teenagers and introduced them as her children. She gushed about their potential for greatness. The teenagers did their best to ignore the display. Nobody liked to see their parents act beneath themselves.

Feeling awkward under her intense gaze, Todd smiled.

The store's only customer left with no purchases in hand.

"Is Mr. Ho here?" Fisk asked.

"Yes. Out back."

Fisk strode to the rear of the store like he knew the layout well and opened the door marked private. The Ho teenagers kept their gazes downcast like eye contact would turn them to stone.

Fisk waited for the door to close before shouting out, "Mr. Ho." He walked through the stock room, examining open boxes containing the unsold items resting in popcorn chips, and calling out Ho's name.

"What are we doing here?" Todd asked.

"Our job. Mr. Ho."

Mr. Ho emerged from a poorly framed box that pretended to be an office. He was small and frail. His clothes hung off him and they made him look older than he was. Todd guessed he was in his late forties carrying a ten-year penalty. Unlike Mrs. Ho, Mr. Ho exhibited no joviality.

"Mr. Fisk," he said, his accent distorting the words. "Good to see you."

"Good to see you again, Mr. Ho. I thought you'd been avoiding me. This is my colleague, Mr. Collins."

Todd didn't like how his name was being bandied about. Fisk was tossing his out too, so Todd guessed no one would be telling tales. This was going to be a town Todd could never return to, that was for sure.

"We've come about—"

"I know," Mr. Ho interrupted. "I'm sorry." He dropped his head.

"You see, Todd, this is the harsh reality of the true American dream." Fisk backed the man into his office. "Mr. Ho here came to this great nation to start a business, to prosper, and he needed money for that. Money that he didn't have. He needed a loan. But as an immigrant, he had no credit record in the US and conventional lines of credit weren't available. That's where Carlson Realty stepped up to the plate. They provided these wonderful premises and a generous loan. But Mr. Ho hasn't been paying back what he owes, have you. Mr. Ho?" Fisk picked up an illustrated jewelry box where the illustration had been an adhesive transfer that had been lacquered over. "And I can see why when you try to sell crap like this. No wonder you have more staff than customers in the store."

Fisk hurled the jewelry box at the ground. It bounced off the concrete floor and broke apart. Mr. Ho flinched at the sight of his merchandise's destruction. Todd felt nauseous all over again.

"I'm expecting a payment of at least three thousand dollars, Mr. Ho. Please tell me you have it, because that interest is killing you."

"Mr. Fisk, if I could hold off paying you for a month, I would be in your debt."

Fisk choked out his derision in the form of a laugh.

"It would give the store a chance to bring in customers."

"I don't think so. I think, Mr. Ho, you have to be taught a lesson about the rules of a free market economy. Todd, don't mark his face. Keep it to the body. I don't want anyone getting curious."

"What?" Todd said. Everything snapped into place. This was

racketeering 101.

Fisk turned his attention away from Mr. Ho to Todd. "I want you to hurt him."

"I think he's got the message."

"Just do as I tell you."

Mr. Ho backed away from the men into the confines of his office. Todd crossed a line he never thought he'd cross and followed Mr. Ho.

The Chinese man, realizing he'd backed himself into a corner, panicked. He searched for a route of escape that would take him past Fisk and Todd. There was none and it only served to fuel his panic. He flailed at the weak walls in hope of bursting through. The walls weren't to code but strong enough to withstand Mr. Ho. Todd closed in on him.

"Body blows only, Todd," Fisk advised.

Mr. Ho whirled around to face Todd. He dropped his arms down as not to provoke a fight. In his native tongue, he pleaded to Todd.

Todd grabbed Mr. Ho by the throat and pinned him to his desk. The man begged for time and consideration. Todd locked gazes with him and saw into him. He felt the man's struggle to attain his dreams and felt them being shattered all at once. Todd raised his fist to strike. Hitting a defenseless man should have been easy, but it was anything but. What possible satisfaction could anyone feel from beating this man? It was no different from pulling the wings from a bug. He couldn't do it and dropped his fist.

"Get out of my way."

Fisk jerked Todd aside. The flicker of relief that appeared on Mr. Ho's face died when Fisk drove a fist into his gut. The blow sounded like a four by two striking a side of beef. It cut Mr. Ho's strings and he crumpled. Only Fisk's steadying hand kept him from crashing to the floor.

Fisk delivered blow after blow, until the man's flesh and spirit surrendered. Todd never challenged Fisk. He didn't fear his own beating, but his interference would have made Mr. Ho's worse. Fisk would have done it out of spite, just to teach Todd a lesson. After Fisk delivered his last punch, he released Mr. Ho and he slid to the floor.

Fisk dropped to one knee and loomed over the Chinese man. "This is the first and last warning to you. I won't ever hurt you like this again. You have two lovely kids out there. You won't if you disappoint me next time. Have my money for me next week."

Mr. Ho wept in reply.

"Both of you have ruined my morning."

Fisk grabbed Todd by the shirt and thrust him out of the store the way they'd come. Mrs. Ho looked confused and asked if something was wrong. Store patronage had swollen to three and they looked just as confused. The kids understood and immediately rushed in the direction of their father.

"A small misunderstanding, Mrs. Ho," Fisk said. "Nothing to worry about." And he shoved Todd out onto the street.

By the time he'd gotten Todd to his car, he'd cooled down. He let go of Todd's shirt, unlocked the doors to his Saab convertible and told him to get in. He drove out to the outskirts of the town to a dingy bar that overlooked the city. The bar wasn't open but Fisk had keys and let them in. He poured two heavy measures of bourbon, never bothering to ask Todd if he drank let alone liked bourbon. He set the glasses down on the bar with the freshly opened bottle.

"I don't know whether to be disappointed or not," Fisk said after knocking back his bourbon.

Todd dodged a response and gulped down half the liquor. He let it burn his insides. He needed to be sanitized.

"You came to kill Carlson, but you couldn't drop a punch on a poor, dumb immigrant."

"You should have warned me."

"It was a test."

"You get to study for a test."

Fisk refreshed their glasses. "Not all tests."

"I failed, I suppose."

"I haven't made up my mind. Pass or fail depends on your perspective. To the Carlsons, you failed. You're no good to them. To your pastor, you passed. You're a good Christian."

"I don't have a pastor."

"You're not the only one." Fisk made short work of his second bourbon. He poured again, noticed where this kind of early morning drinking would lead, and capped the bottle and returned it to its shelf. "What did you really come to Seattle for? You said work, but I don't think so."

"A name of a man in San Francisco. I believe the Carlsons deal with him."

"Deal with him—how?"

"I don't know the details, but he's part of a drug distribution scam. Stolen luxury cars get driven across country carrying shipments of cocaine in the interior."

Fisk made no attempt to deny or confirm the operation. He sipped his bourbon this time.

"What do you want with this person—a job?"

"I've already worked for him. I just want to give notice."

"And you don't know this person's name?"

Todd shook his head.

"You do suck at this game."

"But I'm learning fast."

"I'll take your word for it. Describe your employer."

Todd outlined the small man's description. "Know him?"

Fisk shrugged. "Let me look into it. I'll see what I can dig up."

Todd drank. This time, he let the liquor warm him and not burn him.

"What about Jeff Carlson?" Todd asked.

"What about him?"

"What are you going to tell him about me?"

"Haven't decided, so don't press me. Okay?"

They sat in silence for a while. Each of them was lost in their own thoughts. The silence never became awkward or ugly. Todd broke it when his glass was empty.

"How did you get into this?"

"In a lot of ways it just happened, but I owe my career to one man."

"Jeff Carlson?"

"Hell, no. I owe everything to someone I truly respected. You would have liked him."

"What's his name?"

"Munson. He's dead now."

* * *

Todd made it back to his motel by late afternoon. Fisk had left him to his own devices when the manager came to the bar to open up. Away from anyone that had anything to do with the Carlsons, he'd wandered around the town. He ended up at Gas Works Park, sitting opposite the water watching the boats and rowers wander up and down the Sound. As the sun set, the strip club's boast of hundreds of sexy girls and three ugly ones lured him. He wanted to see just how ugly the ugly ones were. It was the best way to end the day.

But it wasn't to be. The ex-marines were waiting for him in the motel's parking lot. This time, they kept their hands and zip ties to themselves. The ground rules had been set.

Todd didn't ask what they wanted and got into the car with them.

They drove him back to Carlson's office. It was after five and the building had been evacuated, except for the guards on the security desk. People had better things to do. The ex-marines left him at the doors and he checked in with the guards. The guards okayed his arrival and sent him up. Carlson met him at the elevator.

"You had a good first day, Fisk tells me."

So the man had covered for him. Todd didn't know why he should have. Maybe Fisk realized the hole he was in and was giving him a way out. It could have been out of kindness, but Todd guessed it was for more business reasons. He could make a real mess of things if he botched something. Even if Carlson learned the truth about Todd and gave him a bullet severance package, that would still bring Carlson attention he didn't need. Fisk was a guardian angel after all—and not just for the Carlsons.

Carlson led Todd to his office. "Fisk had some ideas on where you can fit in this organization and I'm happy to let that happen."

"Thank you." Todd wasn't really sure what else to say. There was a but coming and he braced himself for it.

Carlson breezed by the unoccupied desks. Even organized crime kept corporate hours these days. He sat down at his desk with the city he ran behind him. Todd sat in the same seat he'd sat in this morning.

"Obviously, your part in this organization is dependent on you passing your probation."

"Jessica?"

Carlson smiled. "Got it in one. Dispose of her and you've got a job for life."

"Like Munson?"

Carlson maintained the smile, but it looked brittle.

"Like Munson," he conceded. "I'm in his debt." The smile fractured and fell away. "And I'll be in yours, if you can get the job done."

"Mr. Carlson, it will be done. By this time next week, Jessica will no longer be a thorn in your side."

And Todd meant it.

* * *

Two days later, Jessica called. In those two days, Todd had done nothing. Fisk covered for him. The word back to Carlson was that he was doing good work. Todd turned tourist and discovered the strip club underestimated the number of ugly girls at their club. He couldn't fault the management for trying. Their marketing ploy had worked. God bless the free market economy.

"Todd, I have something."

Jessica reeled off an address on the waterfront and he met her there. He'd expected a pretty marina setting, but this was where working fisherman worked. She waited for him at a quay in front of a corroded fishing boat.

"What's the plan?" Todd asked.

"A burial at sea."

"I'm going to have a hard time getting him on this boat with you and a gun. I don't know anything about boats. I'm going to need someone to captain this thing and I'm not too keen on witnesses."

"Jeff will drive you out and I'll drive you back."

"Again, there's the problem of keeping you hidden."

"Don't worry. I won't be here. I'll be there." She pointed to a barge floating out in the distance.

Jessica piloted the trawler out to the barge. She explained that the place acted as a nice drop off for their incoming cargo. Not all of it reached the port.

"A floating smuggler's cove," Todd said.

"And a quiet place for a murder."

* * *

"It's done," Todd said.

"What?" Carlson spoke with sleep in his throat.

He'd called Carlson's private phone number. He'd given it to Todd at his office. Apparently the phone was a cell of the pay as you go variety. It would be going in the trash after tonight.

"What you asked, it's done."

"Is it now?" A grin made it down the line. "Come to the office in the morning."

"Do you want to see the body before disposal?"

Carlson pondered that one. Todd knew he couldn't resist. There was too much pent up hate for him not to want to see.

"Sure. Where are you?"

"The barge. Come alone."

"Alone?"

"I don't want people knowing what I did for you. You bring someone, they are going to tell someone. Eventually, it's going to get back to Fisk or someone else with alliances belonging to Jessica. When that happens, it's over for me."

"Okay. Alone it is."

Todd almost felt sorry for the guy.

* * *

Todd waited for two hours in the cold on the barge. The wind and spray cut through his clothes. What was taking so long? He hoped Carlson wasn't shafting him. He couldn't rely on anyone for this to go as planned. Carlson could take this opportunity to take care of him. It was just as easy to dispose of two bodies as it was one. All he could do was hope.

The trawler's engine won the battle with the wind. Todd went to the side of the barge and the boat's spotlight picked him out. He waved back to the boat, his hand tight on the .357.

Carlson brought the boat alongside the barge with practiced ease. He climbed up the rope ladder just as easy.

"How the hell did you get her here?"

Todd used the truth, so he wouldn't screw up the details. The story came out smooth without sounding false. Every convincing lie needed to sit upon a solid foundation of truth to work. "This is where we planned to kill you."

Carlson belted out a laugh. "That's brilliant. I bet she never saw it coming."

"And neither did you," Jessica said back. She emerged from the shadows pointing her automatic. "See what he brought to the party."

Todd jerked out the .357. He approached Carlson with caution. The man bristled with rage.

"Hands up," Todd ordered.

"You sided with her after all I did for you?"

Todd shrugged. "You didn't offer that much and she did ask first. I've got to show some loyalty. Without loyalty, you aren't anything."

"You piece of shit."

Todd relieved Carlson of a Glock. Oddly, it was the only weapon he found on him. Somehow, Todd expected to find a backup.

Todd went behind Carlson and stamped down on the back of his knee. Carlson folded and sprawled face first on the wet, checkerplate decking. Todd stepped on the man's back to keep him from moving. He aimed both guns at Carlson.

"Do it," she said.

Todd didn't look up. He didn't want her seeing the fear.

He looked at Carlson's head twisting to see his and spew expletives. He looked up with contempt and hate, but Todd saw Mr. Ho's face frightened face. When did it become so simple to extinguish a life? What had to be wrong or missing in a person that they could cross the line between person and killer? All Todd knew was that he didn't have it. He aimed his .357 at Jessica. Hers had been on Carlson and she jerked her gun at Todd.

"This is one marital dispute you'll have to sort out between the two of you."

"You gutless bastard," she hissed.

"Yeah, well, at least I know what I am."

"Jessica, you were always a bad judge of character," Carlson berated.

"You don't put a bullet in him," Jessica warned. "I'll put one in you."

"That might be a bit difficult." Todd dropped the Glock on the ground. It landed just out of Carlson's reach. "I'm going to take the boat now. You do whatever you need to do."

"You said you didn't know how to pilot one," Jessica said.

"I'll learn."

"Don't think this lets you off the hook with me," Carlson warned Todd.

"I don't, but it depends who's the quicker on the draw."

Todd eased the pressure on Carlson's back. He squirmed for the Glock. His fingers snagged on the trigger guard. Jessica shifted her aim to Carlson.

"Leave it where it is, Jeff," she warned.

"Good luck," Todd said and bolted for the rope ladder. The quick succession of shots and the order stopped him.

"Put the gun down and turn around."

Todd put his .357 down and turned around. Jessica lay on her back with half her face lost under a mask of blood. Carlson lay face down with the Glock wrapped in his fist and his brains deposited on his back, the shot having gone through the top and out the back of his skull. Fisk stood between the two, casting a glance over his handiwork.

He kicked the gun out of Jessica's dead grasp while keeping his aim on Todd. "I'm glad you didn't go through with it. I didn't want to have to kill you too."

"How did you know we'd be here?"

"Who did you think gave her the idea?" Fisk yanked the Glock from Carlson's grasp and hurled it into the water.

"You and she were in it together, but you killed her?"

"There was a time when I would have killed Jeff for her, but those days are long since gone. I was just playing the game. These two were so focused on getting rid of each other that they never looked outside the goldfish bowl. Help me roll these two into the water."

"Are we cool?" Todd asked.

"Yeah, we're going to be after all this is out of the way. Now pick up your gun, take the bullets out and put them in a pocket, then put the gun away."

Todd did so and helped Fisk weight the Carlsons down and roll them into Puget Sound. Fisk claimed Jessica's automatic and tossed that in after her.

"I'll give you a ride back," Fisk said.

"Why?" Todd asked back aboard the trawler.

Fisk was at the controls. His gun was holstered and no longer a barrier to questions.

"Munson."

"The guy in Florida?"

"He wasn't just run down crossing the street. Jessica and Jeff ordered that. The cops were closing in on him. The Carlsons couldn't take a chance, but Munson wouldn't have talked. It wasn't his way. It was a shitty decision for a guy that everyone owed." Fisk went quiet after that.

"You used me." Todd put no malice on the statement.

"Yeah. Word had just gotten back to me that Munson's accident was no accident and I knew then I would take care of Jessica and Jeff. I was looking for a way and when you fell into my lap, you were too good a tool not to use."

"But not a tool you want to keep around."

"No." Fisk smiled. "You've got things to do and I can't use a guy like you."

"Fair enough."

They moored the boat up and Fisk walked Todd to his Toyota.

"The name you wanted," Fisk said. "You want it?"

Did he? It was a good question. This was all getting to be a little much just to get back at the small man. It was stretching him in directions he wasn't used to or wanted to get used to. But the small man wasn't going to go away until Todd stopped him or died trying. Dying. He hadn't thought this would cost him his life, but it was the small man's end game and Todd would have to keep playing until someone won.

"Yeah."

"Leo Cochrane. That's your small man."

Leo Cochrane. Todd ran his mind over the name. He didn't know what to feel at this point. He felt only as if he had learned a fact like any other fact. Nothing would feel good until he had disposed of the small man.

"I'll throw in a bonus name too. Jeremiah Black."

"Who's that?"

"Leo's competition. You might find him a useful wedge."

"How will I get to them?"

"That's for you to work out."

Fisk put out a hand. Todd took it and shook. There was strength and friendship in Fisk's tight grip and Todd returned it.

"Don't ever think about returning to Washington. You're a loose end and you can dangle anywhere but here. Got me?"

Todd nodded. "I'll leave tonight."

"Good. Now piss off."

Fisk went to leave, but Todd stopped him.

"One more favor?"

"You're pushing your luck."

"I know, but I'm repaying a favor to someone."

"Okay."

"There's a dealership in Dallas where you send stolen cars with coke in them. The dealership is called Ruskin's."

"What of it?"

"Forget that it exists."

"Consider it forgotten."

"Thanks."

Fisk pulled out a cell phone and made a call for a pickup. Todd guessed it would be a busy night. Everyone had to be prepped on the new power structure before the start of the next business day.

Todd gunned the Toyota's engine. It struggled in the Seattle cold. He let the car warm up. Fisk came around to the window.

"Where to now?" he asked.

"Home."

PART FIVE
THE SMALL MAN

The Bay Area felt different to Todd. Colors were vibrant. Even the air smelled different. Someone had played with the controls while he'd been away. Had the Bay Area changed or was it he who'd changed? Regardless of the changes, Todd felt good to be home.

He didn't hide. There was no need to take precautions as yet. Cochrane wouldn't be expecting him to return and Todd had no allies in the Bay Area that he would know. He liked the idea of hiding in plain sight. It was a small victory he could celebrate.

He drove by his old apartment in El Cerrito to find the place had been cleaned out. He'd expected as much. He wasn't back to rake over old coals. This was fresh start time—as soon as Cochrane was taken care of. And there was no better time to start.

He parked his road weary Toyota at El Cerrito Plaza. It reminded him of the faithful horses of the Pony Express that had galloped their guts out until they dropped and the rider simply switched to a fresh horse. Sadly for the Toyota, that day was close. The detour back to Texas had sealed the car's fate. Todd had stopped to pick up the cocaine in the bus station locker. The coke would be a useful bargaining chip for Todd. He could trade it, sell it or plant it to bring Cochrane down. How sweet would it be to skewer him with his own junk?

Getting to Cochrane was the problem though. It had occurred to him on his drive from Texas to the Bay Area how unfamiliar he was with Cochrane. Other than the chop shop, he knew nothing about him or his operations. He needed someone who could inject him into Cochrane's world and that person was John "Felix" Katts. He parked up and called Katts on his cell.

"Yeah." Katts seemed to have put all his worldly energy into that one word and still came up short. It was just the sort of response Todd expected for a Saturday afternoon.

"Felix, it's me."

"Jesus, is that you, Todd?" Katts was wild awake now. "Fuck, we all thought you were dead."

"And I'd like to keep it that way."

"Does this have anything to do with the two apes that came sniffing around the factory?"

"What apes?"

"They weren't cops, that's for sure." Katts described Cochrane's gorillas, Dalton and Vasquez. "They swung by twice to see if anyone had talked with you and they weren't too frightened about leaning on anyone who didn't talk up."

"They been by lately?"

"Nah. Your job's toast, by the way. I went by your place too. The manager cleaned it out, the bastard. Ebayed your good shit and Goodwilled the rest."

"No great loss," Todd said and meant it. There was a time when his crappy jobs and apartment defined him, but not anymore. If he had Cochrane to thank for anything, it was that. He'd shown him a future where possibilities could exist. He had no idea what he was going to do once he'd dealt with Cochrane but he wouldn't be punching a clock. "Like I say, I want everyone to think I'm dead."

"Are you in deep shit?"

"Yeah, but I'm climbing out. Can I come by? I need your help."

Understandably, Katts hemmed and hawed, but agreed after a little pressure from Todd. Todd drove out to the duplex Katts rented in Rockridge. Although he lived a block from the rejuvenated Oakland suburb with its fancy restaurants and pretty boutiques, the duplex was an earth tremor away from demolition.

"What do you need, man?" Katts asked, after checking the street to make sure no one was scoping out the place and closing the drapes.

"It's cool, Felix," Todd said. "I'm not being tailed."

"Yeah, yeah, right. Come in."

Todd followed Katts into the living room. Katts lived how Todd expected. He forwent furniture and all modern conveniences so that he could support his extracurricular activity of trying every drug known to illegal medical science. General consensus was that Katts would smoke kitty litter if he believed he'd get a hit off it. Todd sank into a disheveled futon across from Katts' beloved La-Z-Boy.

"Do you need something?" Katts asked. "I've got a couple of cold ones in the fridge."

"No, I'm good."

Katts tossed out more hospitality until Todd stopped him. It was a delaying tactic. Todd felt Katts' apprehension. He wasn't the sharpest tool, but he'd guessed Todd wanted something less than kosher from him.

"So what do you need?"

"Answers to some questions, Felix."

Katts shrugged. "If I can."

"Do you know a guy called Leo Cochrane?"

"No."

"Jeremiah Black?"

"No times two."

This wasn't going the way Todd had hoped, but it was expected. Katts bought drugs and occasionally sold part of his stash to friends when his funds ran short. He didn't run with San Francisco's drug elite.

"Is that it?" Katts asked.

"Pretty much."

"I hate to ask, but who are they?"

"Heavy weight drug dealers."

That lit Katts up. He leapt to his feet, pouring out a string of curses. He leaned over Todd pinning him to his spot on the futon. Todd put his hands up in defense.

"Okay. I like weed and pills, and I've freebased once, but I'm not an addict. Look, do you see tracks?" Katts offered his unmarked arms for inspection. "Do you see?"

"Yeah, I see, Felix. You're clean."

"Damn straight, Todd." Too angry to speak, Katts turned away from Todd and fell into his La-Z-Boy. This simple act took the sting out of him. "I know what everyone thinks and says about me. I know I'm a joke to most people, but I don't find it funny."

"Sorry, Felix."

"Yeah, well, it doesn't fucking matter, does it?"

Todd hadn't expected this reaction and felt bad. It was true what he said though. He was the butt of the jokes everyone told in the lunchroom.

"I didn't mean it to sound the way it did," Todd said. "I came to you because you know people, not because you're a junkie."

Katts failed to look impressed and sulked.

"The reason the apes came looking for me is that I've pissed off Leo Cochrane and I'm trying to square things. Jeremiah Black is someone who might be able to help. I'm wondering if any of the people you know might be able to help me hook up with Black or give me some info on Cochrane."

Katts ran a hand over his shaven head. "I might be able to help. I deal with a guy for X. He's no bottom feeder. He knows people. I'm guessing these guys you want are hardcore. My guy won't be on their level, but he might get you to the next. Sound good?"

"More than good."

"Come back tonight, late. I'll take you to him."

* * *

The house party in the Oakland hills was jumping. At least a hundred people packed a vast, two-story house in a new development not far from the Claremont Hotel. It looked to be a house warming for a young couple. Katts cut a swath through the people and Todd followed in his wake.

Katts stopped a guy dancing with a hot Hispanic girl in a low cut top that drew the eye. Over the sound system, Todd couldn't hear what was being said. Katts thanked the guy who was only too glad to get back to his girl.

"He's upstairs," Katts said to Todd.

They found Katts' dealer in a guest bathroom. He sat on the toilet with his wares spread out on his lap. Three eager guys and a girl, who had yet to graduate, stood with money in their fists. He played to his audience with a nice line of patter, but he cut the patter short when he saw Katts. He took their money and handed out prepackaged pills in tiny plastic bags.

"Tell your friends about Mickey," he said as the foursome filed out.

One of the guys flashed Todd and Katts a baleful look that Todd guessed was the guy's tough guy look. A month ago it would have mattered to Todd. Now, who cared?

"Hey, Felix, how's it going?" Mickey said. "Is this your friend?"

"I'm good, Mickey. Yeah, this is Todd."

Todd and Mickey exchanged nods. Mickey seemed to appraise Todd with his. Todd felt as if he'd just been X-rayed.

"Let's take this outside," Mickey said.

Mickey was mid to late twenties, tall and skinny. He talked tough, but one good punch would fell him like a tree. The glasses, with their cool looking frames, and the Xbox geek face helped his image. If Mickey worked crowds like this one, he was the perfect person to service them. He kept people in their comfort zones.

They retreated to the backyard. The fall chill kept people in the house, although a couple were fooling around somewhere in the darkness, judging by the grunting sounds. Mickey found a spot he liked where the patio lights failed to reach. They were silhouettes in the night, voices in the dark. If no one saw them or heard them, then it never happened.

"You want to know about Jeremiah Black?" Mickey asked.

"And Leo Cochrane," Todd said.

"I don't know him."

"But you know Jeremiah?"

"Look, I'm a foot soldier. I receive orders and I follow them. The Jeremiah Blacks of this world don't come down to my level. I know his rep and you'd be better off not pushing this any further."

It was impossible to ignore the note of panic building in Mickey's voice. Black sounded mean. That was good. If Todd was going to topple Cochrane then he needed someone like Jeremiah Black doing some of the pushing for him.

"I don't have a choice," Todd said. "I need to meet Black."

Mickey shifted his weight from one foot to the other. His nervousness spread to Katts.

"Maybe you should listen to him, Todd, man," Katts said.

"I wish I could. If you can't help, Mickey, that's cool. No harm, no foul as far as I'm concerned, but I have to get to Black one way or another."

Mickey shook his head and sighed. "I can help. I'm not saying I can't. I just want you to know the risks."

"Duly noted. I'll make it worth Black's while."

"How?" Mickey asked.

"That's for Black to know, but you can pass it on to him that I can help his empire flourish more than it already does."

Mickey cast another appraising gaze over Todd. "Serious?"

"Serious."

"Okay. I know someone who's close to Black. I'll see if I can get you a meet."

"Thanks," Todd said. "I appreciate it."

"You should. This is going to cost me a lot of favors. I'm only doing this because Felix is a friend and a good customer."

Mickey came through on the following Monday. Todd got a call from Katts in the morning saying to be at Scala's Bistro in San Francisco at seven. A reservation would be in Todd's name. The news made Todd feel sick to his stomach, but he thanked Katts for his help.

"Todd, don't take this the wrong way, but I'd like it if you forgot all about me."

"Sure, Felix."

Katts ended the call.

Todd was on his own again. It was probably for the best. Things were bound to get messy from now on. It wasn't fair to drag people like Katts and Mickey into it any more than necessary.

The Scala's Bistro thing worried him. It was an odd place to meet. It was visible, for one. They'd be seen. It was safe though. It wasn't like Black could shoot him in a public place and not have some of the drama splash back on him. Of course, they'd done that in a hundred gangster movies. This wasn't the movies, but it wasn't far off. There was nothing he could do but play by Black's rules.

Todd had checked into a rundown motel in San Pablo. The place was relatively clean and their weekly rates were low, but their main selling point was they took anonymous cash. He hung out there until it was time for his appointment with Black. Scala's was attached to the Sir Francis Drake Hotel. A pair of beefeaters guarded the hotel's main entrance and carried in arriving and departing guests' bags. He arrived early. They couldn't seat him yet, so he sat at the bar. He was on his second beer when the hostess fetched him and led him to his table at the rear of the restaurant. A waiter arrived within the mandated ninety seconds of seating and fussed, but Todd sent him packing with a curt remark.

Seven p.m. came and went without Black's arrival. Todd caved to the waiter's repeated visits and ordered an appetizer he didn't want.

Todd knew what was going on. Black was testing him. He didn't know who Todd was and he probably used all day to check him out. Having found nothing that made the radar, they'd force him to wait it out. He was probably being watched at this moment. He scanned the diners and the wait staff for someone paying too much attention to his table. Black's people were good. He didn't spot anyone. Still, he didn't feel he was in safe hands and his anxiety grew with every passing minute.

At seven fifty, the hostess approached with a young African American man dressed in a tailored business suit that made him look like a newscaster. The man smiled when he reached the table. He put out a hand and said, "Mr. Collins, it's good to see you again."

"Likewise, Mr. Black." Todd rose and shook hands. Black's hand was cool and dry.

When the hostess left and they'd given their order to the irritating waiter, Black said, "Not what you were expecting, am I?"

"To be honest, I don't know what to expect these days. Life's been like that lately. But to answer your question, no."

"Regardless of my product, I'm a businessman. I want to sell to as many consumers as possible. That means I have to deal with people from the cream to the dregs and that requires me to be a chameleon. I have a degree in business from a well-respected UC college and I speak fluent Ebonics. I can be anything I need to be. I thought you might like this environment."

"Not really my thing."

"So I understand. I thought it would make a nice change for you." Black snapped open his napkin and rested it across his lap. "You need to leave, now."

"What?"

"Room two-ten. Now. I need to see if you're fucking me or not."

They were waiting for him, three of them. Whereas Black claimed to be a chameleon, these guys couldn't boast the same. They were predators. One of them introduced himself as Kenneth and he ordered the other two to strip him and look for a wire. Todd was glad he'd left the .357 in the Toyota. One of them barked at him to put his clothes back on.

"Can I go?"

"Mr. Black told us to give you this," Kenneth said and slammed a fist into Todd's gut.

Todd deflated, collapsing to his knees. He held his stomach, half expecting to find a hole there.

"He says, keep things on the level," Kenneth said.

Todd nodded. It was about the only thing he could do.

Black's men saw themselves out.

It was another ten minutes before Todd rejoined Black in the restaurant.

"I told them to keep your salad in the kitchen," Black remarked like nothing had happened.

Todd said nothing.

"Hey, don't take it so personally. You know I had to check."

The waiter deposited Todd's salad before him and departed.

"So what is it you want, Todd?"

"Do you know Leo Cochrane?"

Black speared an heirloom tomato and nodded.

"Leo doesn't like me breathing. I want to change that."

"Leo wants you dead. So what?"

"The guy tried to set me up and I got wise to it. I'd like to return the favor."

"Again, so what?"

"I thought you'd be interested in helping me. It would be in your interest. With Leo out of the way, his clients become your clients.

You said you're a businessman. Doesn't a hostile takeover sound good to a businessman?"

Black put his fork down and pushed his plate away from him. "You want me to become your triggerman? I ice Leo for you and all your problems disappear." He paused for Todd to comment. Todd didn't. "Do I look fucking stupid? If I kill Leo, that brings a bunch of unwanted heat down on me. There's nothing there for me. Leo kills you. Who cares? Leo will carry on. I will carry on. The world will carry on. There's no incentive for me. Although, I could buy myself a few points with Leo by selling you out to him."

Todd swallowed. He'd made a mistake. Black was going to hang him out to dry.

"But that can change," Black said.

"How?"

"What have you got to offer me?"

"Six kilos of cocaine. Leo was using it to set me up. I kept it."

"That's a lot of blow. Got any of it with you?"

"In my car."

"I think we should take a look at it."

They finished their meal. Black handed Todd the check. Well, it was Todd's date after all.

He walked Black to his Toyota at a nearby parking garage. Black's backup followed in a Dodge Magnum. They parked behind Todd's Toyota, boxing him in and giving the transaction some privacy. Todd popped the trunk and unzipped the backpack letting Black see one of the six kilo packets.

"I thought you said you had six kilos."

"I do," Todd said, "but I saw no reason why I should bring them all."

Black stepped back and snapped his fingers at Kenneth. He took the packet from Todd, slit it open with a switchblade and brought out a sample of the cocaine on the tip of the blade. He tasted some and rubbed some between his fingers before nodding at Black.

"Looks as if you've got something."

"So are you in?" Todd asked. "Will you help?"

Black pondered. Todd felt he'd already made up his mind and this was a performance for his crew.

"No."

Todd felt slapped. "What?"

"Six kilos of free blow is nice but not nice enough. You're on your own."

Todd went to say, "you can't." But Black could. This wasn't his fight, so why get involved? Todd decided Black was a good businessman.

"I think I'll keep this." Black took the coke from Kenneth. "Call it dessert. That okay with you?"

Kenneth eased back his leather jacket to let Todd see his Tec-9 machine pistol.

"It's the least I can do."

Black smiled and got into the back of the Dodge. His crew fell in behind him. Black powered down the window. "Good luck, brother, because you're going to need it."

Todd shrugged.

"If you can bring me something better than another five of these—" Black held up the coke, "—I'm willing to listen. Seriously. Okay?"

Todd nodded and watched the Dodge drive off. He supposed he should have felt pissed, but he didn't. He didn't want the drugs around him in the first place. Besides, this was the price of doing business. He still had more than enough coke left to use against Cochrane.

He left the parking garage and threaded his way back to the Bay Bridge. With the never-ending bridge construction, getting to the bridge these days was an epic quest that sent the driver twice around the city before access could be granted to an on-ramp. Todd was turning right onto Harrison when a Malibu rear-ended him. The impact jolted Todd's Toyota into traffic.

"Son of a bitch," Todd groaned.

He waited for the light to change, then made his right and pulled into a parking lot with signs proclaiming "For Authorized Personnel Only."

The driver of the Malibu followed into the parking lot. He popped out of the car and put his hands to his face when he saw the damage to Todd's car.

"I'm sorry, man," he said. "I totally misjudged my braking."

"Yeah, well," Todd said. He was more pissed at the inconvenience than the damage. Besides, he'd never invested in any insurance for the Toyota. The damage to his car was pretty bad. The bumper dangled and the impact had caved in the back to the extent that it popped the trunk lid.

"Look, I was about to scrap this car." Todd attempted to reattach the plastic bumper. "I don't want to go through insurance."

"And I don't want to shoot you." The driver had come in close, jammed a gun in Todd's ribs and forced him against the trunk.

"Just take my wallet. Take the car if you want."

The driver ground the gun hard against Todd's ribs to shut him up. Todd complied.

"What were you doing with Jeremiah Black?"

Oh God, Todd thought. *Who the hell have I upset this time and more importantly, which side does he play for?*

"Nothing."

The driver bounced Todd's head off the Toyota's trunk. "Try again."

"What makes you think I'm going to tell you?" Having his head bounced off the trunk pissed him off. He wasn't about to be taken for a ride twice in one night and he wasn't about to sell Black out to just anyone. He wanted some answers first.

The driver reached inside his pocket and filled Todd's vision with a San Francisco Police Department's detective shield.

"Oh, shit," Todd murmured.

* * *

"And you expect me to believe that pile of horseshit?" Redfern asked.

But he did. Todd watched the gears working in the detective's head as he spoke. A plan was forming in Redfern's brain. Todd wouldn't be going to jail tonight. If he worked this right, he might have just found the backup he needed to go after Cochrane.

They were sitting in Redfern's car a few blocks from the parking lot Todd had stopped in. Todd's battle weary Toyota still sat in the parking lot with the doors unlocked, the key in the ignition and the .357 sitting in the glove box.

"I know it seems crazy," Todd said.

"That's a word for it."

"But it's all true." Admittedly, Todd had kept a number of the details from Redfern. He'd muted his encounters with Moran, Charlie and the Carlsons. It would only create clutter.

"So what are you expecting to get out of this?" Redfern asked.

"Freedom. Cochrane has already shown me that his reach exceeds mine. Unless I do something to put him down, I'll always be looking over my shoulder."

"Put him down? Are you thinking of killing him?"

Todd wasn't sure how he should answer. Redfern was a cop after all, but Todd saw the hunger in his eyes. He wanted a big score and Cochrane might just fit the bill.

"I don't know what I'm thinking," Todd said. "It might come down to that."

"Is that why you met with Jeremiah Black? You thought you'd use his muscle to get the job done, is that it?"

"Something like that," Todd conceded.

"You know how to pick your friends, don't you?" Redfern shook his head. "And what was that he took from your trunk?"

Todd said nothing.

"Have it your way. You told me Cochrane planted six kilos of coke on you. If you don't turn six kilos over to my custody, I'll know where to find the rest."

"So where does this leave us?" Todd asked.

"I don't know. You present a number of interesting possibilities, but it's just as easy to turn you in for a quick bust."

Redfern was trying to scare Todd, but he wasn't buying it. That look of hunger on his face was still there. Redfern needed Todd. He wouldn't get voted off the island this week.

"Help me bring down Leo Cochrane," Todd said.

A police unit blew by with its lights and sirens going. Redfern watched its passing with professional interest. He was a bulldog of a man, but a tired one at that. Muscle had given way to fat, but Todd had no fears that if Redfern wanted to knock him down, he wouldn't get up in a hurry. If it weren't for the badge, Todd wouldn't have believed Redfern was a cop. The hunger he'd seen in Redfern was a product of desperation. He looked like a gambler on a long losing streak. The man was a burnout. Given the choice, Todd would have preferred a different partner.

Redfern gunned the Malibu's engine. "I'm going to check you out. Where are you staying?"

Todd told him. "Aren't you frightened I'm going to run?"

"Where are you going to run? You told me Cochrane would find you wherever you go. You need me."

"And if I check out, then what?"

"Then you're bait."

* * *

Redfern left Todd on the street. It was a cheap play. No doubt a demonstration to show who was in charge. Todd let him play his games. He found his car just as he'd left it, .357 and all. He thanked whoever was watching over him and drove back to his motel. He found Redfern waiting for him in the parking lot in front of his room.

So leaving Todd on the street wasn't such a cheap play after all. Redfern just wanted a head start.

"It didn't take you long to make up your mind," Todd said, unlocking the door to his room.

"I'm a fast thinker," Redfern remarked.

Todd flicked on the lights and the TV. The walls were thin and he didn't want to be overheard.

"Can I see the coke?"

"It's not here. It's in a luggage locker in the city," Todd said. It wasn't. The coke was under the bed, but it wouldn't be by morning. It would be in a luggage locker. The stuff was drawing too many flies.

"What if I were to check the contents of the toilet tank?" Redfern asked with a smirk.

"Be my guest, but you'd only find water."

Redfern checked the tank and a couple of other places, but gave up before he looked under the bed. "I want to see it tomorrow."

Todd sat on the end of the bed. "Okay."

"Got anything to drink around here?" Redfern asked, looking about the room.

Todd's stomach clenched. Did Redfern have a problem? He

hadn't smelled booze on his breath in the car or the telltale cover up smell of Altoids. He hoped to Christ Redfern wasn't a drunk. Chances of success just took a nosedive if he was. "There's the water in the toilet tank."

"Ha, ha, very funny."

"So what's the plan?"

Redfern sat in a threadbare chair that represented the only other place to sit. It sagged under his weight. "Cochrane doesn't know you're here?"

"No."

"You're going to tell him that you are. You're going to tell him that you've got his coke and you'd like to give it back. In return, you want to be off his shit list."

"Sounds tricky," Todd said. It sounded more than that. It sounded lethal. But it also sounded like the only way.

"You'll be wired for sound and videotaped."

"And where will San Francisco PD be when this exchange happens?"

"I won't be far away. You'll be totally safe."

"Only if you can travel faster than a speeding bullet, because if Cochrane pulls a gun, I'm screwed."

"For this to work, you have to be seen giving the drugs back and Cochrane needs to acknowledge that they were his in the first place. You'll be in good hands. It's not like we're breaking new ground here. There have been plenty of operations like this."

"Sounds like a cakewalk."

"Hey, watch the mouth."

Todd brushed the warning aside. "Don't you think Cochrane will check me for a wire, weapons and undercover cops?"

"That's why we'll test the waters tomorrow." Redfern pushed himself free of the chair. "Meet me outside the Metreon tomorrow, the 4th Street side, at eleven. You're going to give Leo a call."

* * *

Todd found Redfern standing under the vertical neon sign for the Metreon. He'd stashed the remaining five kilos of Cochrane's cocaine in a locker and it felt good not to have it in his possession again.

"You're late," Redfern said.

"I slept in."

Redfern took him inside the complex and bought coffees. They sat at a table in an unoccupied area of the dining section. The lunchtime crowd had yet to arrive.

"I've been doing some checking up," Redfern said.

"And?"

"Paul Helfers, the drug dealer you had that fender bender with, hasn't been seen since the traffic stop."

"That's because he's in a hole in the ground a thousand miles from here. So you believe me now?"

"Let's say your story has some credibility. What makes me like it more is that when we bust Cochrane for the drugs, we can tack on a murder rap."

"Well, I do know where the body is buried."

Redfern fished in his pocket and handed Todd a scrap of paper with a number on it.

"What's this?"

"Leo Cochrane's private cell phone number."

"How'd you get that?"

"Police work. Now listen."

Redfern walked Todd through the call to Cochrane. He provided Todd with a cover story for how he got the number and the line he was going to feed Cochrane. Redfern made him rehearse. There was no judging what Cochrane would say exactly but there were likely outcomes. Redfern changed the script every time to counter for the possible scenarios. They role-played for an hour until Redfern was satisfied Todd sounded genuine enough to make the call.

"Ready?" the detective asked.

"About as ready as I'm ever going to get."

They left the Metreon and searched for a phone booth, which proved harder than it should. With so many cell phones out in the public domain, phone booths were a dying breed. They found one in the lobby of the Moscone Center and Redfern handed Todd a phone card.

"I don't want you running out of quarters."

Todd took out Cochrane's number from his pocket and the nerves hit. Until now, he'd been feeling cool and calm about the call. Cochrane couldn't harm him while they talked on the phone. He was untouchable. But now his stomach clenched and he had an overwhelming desire to take a leak. Cochrane was connected. He could get to anyone. He was the bogeyman. Todd was screwed.

"What are you waiting for?" Redfern demanded.

"Nothing," Todd said and punched in the number.

The phone rang for a long time. Todd thought it was going to switch to voicemail when it was answered.

"Yes."

It was Cochrane. Todd's legs went weak, but as the adrenaline flowed, his fear evaporated.

"Remember me, Leo?"

There was silence, but it wasn't from confusion. Cochrane had recognized Todd's voice. Todd felt his surprise coming down the line.

"That sounds like my friend Todd."

"I didn't know we were friends. Especially after the wild goose chase you sent me on."

"You know what they say, you only hurt the ones you love. How'd you get this number?"

"Know a guy called Ruiz?"

"That piece of shit. Remind me to squash that bug."

"I'll do that."

"You sound edgy, Todd."

"Understandable, don't you think?"

Redfern, eager for feedback, motioned to Todd. Todd gave him the thumbs up.

"Are you close?" Cochrane asked.

"I'm in the city."

"We should meet."

"Under the circumstances, you'll understand if I'm not too eager."

"Fair enough. Why don't you tell me what you want?"

"I want to be off your shit list."

"What makes you think you're on it?"

"Don't piss about. I've been reading up. I know how important Paul Helfers was to you and you iced him and stuffed him in the back of a Lexus. That was my fault. You aren't going to forget it in a hurry."

"If I remember, when we last spoke, you weren't too kind to me."

"Yeah, well, I'm sorry. I didn't really know how big a hole I was in and at the time, I was angry. I thought I was working off my debt, but you were setting me up."

"I was angry too. Maybe I was overzealous. I certainly under-estimated you."

"Likewise."

Todd took a second to assess his performance. Cochrane sounded like he was taking the bait, so far. Todd didn't put it down to his acting or Redfern's coaching abilities. The script had gone out the window. There were no lies or deceptions at work. He was speak-ing from the heart.

"Look," Todd said, "I know how much I cost you."

"You have no idea how much you cost me."

"I think I do—a dead body, a gun and six kilos of coke. The body and the gun told me enough and throwing in a little coke was overkill, but six kilos—that's a vendetta."

"Like I say, I was overzealous. Heat of the moment stuff. But I'm listening now. How are you proposing to heal the rift?"

"The blow. I should have thrown it out, but I kept it. I don't know its street value, but it can't be cheap. You can't afford to be throwing away that kind of money. I'll return it and then we're quits. Agreed?"

Cochrane paused for effect. It was to make Todd sweat. Todd knew this because he was sweating up a storm.

"You've thought this out." The suspicious note in Cochrane's voice was difficult to ignore.

"I've had plenty of time to do it. Living the underground life teaches you what's important."

Cochrane laughed. "Been having a hard time of it, Todd? Well, it's not a lifestyle that suits everyone. Okay, Todd, I like you. Give me back my coke and you're a free man. Remember the shop in Oakland where you picked up the Lexus? Come there in an hour."

Redfern flashed him a hand signal to wind things up.

"I don't think so."

"You don't trust me?"

"I like the idea of neutral ground with plenty of witnesses."

"You have come a long way. Have it your way, Todd. When and where?"

"I'll call with instructions," Todd said and hung up. He sagged and leaned against the lobby wall before his legs gave out.

Redfern grinned. The grin took years off him. "Very nice. I couldn't have done better myself."

"I have a real incentive to make this work."

"C'mon, let's get out of here. I doubt Cochrane was linked up to anything to trace the number, but I don't want to take any chances."

The phone on the wall rang. Todd and Redfern froze.

"Him?" Todd asked.

"Just trying his luck." Redfern picked up the phone and dropped it back down on the cradle. "C'mon."

Outside the Moscone Center, Redfern talked Todd through the arrangements for tomorrow's sting. It sounded straightforward enough. Well, as straightforward as anything that had happened to Todd in the last month.

"I'll see you tonight," Redfern said.

"Where are you going?"

"Where do you think? These operations don't just appear. There's a lot of preparation." He fished in his pocket and handed Todd a key and another scrap of paper with an address on it.

"What's this?"

"Keys to a safe house. Not exactly a safe house. They're keys to my place. I want you there. Now that I've got you, I don't want anything happening to you. Check out of that motel and hole up at my place. I don't want you out there advertising you're back in town."

Now the machine was in motion. It would be all over by tomorrow.

Redfern called an apartment at a four-unit, three-story townhouse on the edge of Noe Valley home. Individual garages occupied the first floor and the apartments the second and third. The exterior paint job the color of boiled-cabbage sapped the building of its art deco charm. Todd parked the Toyota on the street and went inside.

The interior was exactly what Todd expected. It resembled Redfern's appearance—shabby and neglected. Takeout containers filled the trash and towered on the kitchen dish drainer. The bed in the apartment's only bedroom looked as if someone had danced on it in their boots. The neglect carried over to the other rooms as well. The absence of a woman's touch was obvious, but a photo above the fireplace of a woman with two teenage boys painted the picture of a broken marriage.

Poor bastard, Todd thought. *Never thought I'd find someone worse off than me.*

He dumped his meager possessions on the floor next to the pullout sofa, but kept the .357 on him. He took out the trash and tried tidying up, but it was a job for a professional. He couldn't bum around all day in this place waiting for Redfern to return, especially when there was nothing to eat or drink. He locked up and went in search of groceries.

On 24th Street, he found an overpriced specialty market, but for once, it didn't hurt his bankroll. He still had plenty of cash left over from his various jobs he'd picked up. He and Redfern wouldn't eat like kings tonight, but they would eat food that didn't feature delivery.

On the walk back to Redfern's apartment, Todd played the next twenty-four hours through his head. There was little for him to do now. He would simply hand over the coke and Redfern and the SFPD would do the rest. Obviously, Cochrane could ice him on the spot, but if he got him to say the magic words right off the bat, there wouldn't be time. Still, he wished the cops weren't involved. Redfern had yet to tell him where he stood in all this. He'd disposed of a body. That made him an accessory after the fact or something. And that seemed to be the least of his crimes. No matter how he sliced it, there were going to be charges of some sort.

"Hey, Todd."

Reflexively and stupidly, Todd turned towards the voice behind him. Before he could utter a word, a fist drove into his solar plexus. He dropped to his knees, the grocery sacks spilling from his grasp. All attempts to cry out for help ended in a strangled squeak. Thoughts of reaching for his gun never even materialized.

The owner of the fist dropped to one knee, as if to help. He snatched a fistful of Todd's tee shirt and jerked him up to his ear. "It's your unlucky day, dickhead," he rasped and jammed a 9mm automatic in Todd's gut.

He guided Todd to his feet and spun him around. He felt for a weapon and found the .357 in the back of Todd's pants.

"I'll take that. Not like it was yours in the first place."

Todd recognized his captor. It was Dalton, the black linebacker Cochrane had brought with him to Todd's apartment. His sidekick, Vasquez, sat at the wheel of a Lincoln across the street. The linebacker bundled him into the back of the car. He slammed Todd twice with the butt of the .357 and that was it. Todd was out cold.

* * *

Todd came to while they were on the road. His wrists were cuffed behind him. He lay face down in the foot well for the rear passengers. Dalton's feet pressed down on Todd's back pinning him in place.

"He's awake," Dalton said. "Enjoy these minutes, Todd. They are your last."

The comedians laughed.

Todd didn't bother asking where he was going. He didn't want to know.

The Lincoln came to a halt inside a building. Todd listened to the clatter of a garage door closing. He knew they'd taken him back to the chop shop at Jack London Square. The linebackers yanked him from the back of the car. This time, the place had been cleaned out of vehicles and equipment. In the middle of the shop sat Cochrane on an uncomfortable looking tubular steel and wood chair with a fixed back. Next to him laid a body bag. And next to that sat a bucket. He rested a silenced pistol lazily on his lap. These simple props and the stark surroundings struck fear into Todd. No explanation was necessary. All that was needed was a meager imagination to construct a scenario. This was where he was going to die. There was just time enough to lament how close he'd come to winning this one.

Cochrane stood and pointed to the chair. The strength went out of Todd's legs and the linebackers had to drag him over to it. They planted him in the seat. His head sagged under its own weight. Cochrane lifted it with the pistol.

"I never thought you were stupid enough to come back, Todd. Honestly, I didn't," Cochrane said. "After I sent you on your way to Dallas and you didn't end up in custody, I put the word out on you. I expected to receive a call from some corner of this country to tell me you'd ridden into town and they'd taken care of business.

I thought the coke would bring you down. I was sure you'd try to hustle it. Do you really have it?"

Todd swallowed. His Adam's apple nudged the end of the silencer. "Yes."

Cochrane forced the pistol hard against Todd's throat. "Honestly?"

All saliva escaped down Todd's throat and it burned when he answered, "Honestly."

"You wouldn't be lying?" Todd went to answer, but Cochrane shushed him. "I wouldn't blame you if you were. Stronger men than you have when faced with this predicament."

"No."

"I think I believe you. The question is, is it worth the bother of getting it back?"

Dalton had wandered around behind Todd positioning himself in Todd's blind spot. Cochrane nodded to him. He upended the chair, pitching Todd onto his knees then his face. Cochrane jerked Todd back and shoved the bucket under his face. Vasquez held his face over the bucket and Cochrane pressed the pistol against the back of his head.

"I don't know anyone who does this. I fill the bucket halfway with water. When I shoot you, the bucket will catch the spattered remains of your face and the water will stop the bullet from ricocheting off the walls. You wouldn't believe how much this saves on cleanup."

Todd stared at his reflection. This was the last thing he'd see: his terrified expression before Cochrane's bullet ripped it to pieces. He tried to close his eyes, but fear kept them wide open.

"Where's my coke? And please don't waste my time."

Todd answered before he even comprehended what he'd said. His survival instinct had reacted on pure reflex and answered for him. It had bought him time. Even a second chance.

"Show me," Cochrane said.

* * *

Todd traveled with Cochrane and his two linebackers in the Lincoln. This time, they let him sit up. Still cuffed, he sat on the backseat with Dalton and his angry looking hand cannon. Vasquez pulled up across the street from Redfern's Noe Valley apartment.

Todd searched the street for his lucky talisman and he found it. Redfern's battered Malibu was parked on the street. Redfern was home and that was good. The trick was warning him that he was bringing company for dinner.

"I'm at this place over here," Todd said.

"Better than your old place," Cochrane remarked.

"I wasn't planning on staying long."

"Make him presentable."

Dalton turned Todd around and uncuffed him. The respite from the cuffs' bite was temporary. Dalton re-cuffed Todd's hands in front of him and covered them up with a jacket. Suitably camouflaged to the world, they led him over to the apartment.

"Keys," Cochrane said at the top of the apartment's marble stairs. *C'mon, Redfern, please be watching the windows. Please be primed and ready.* Todd wished he and Redfern had agreed on some secret entry code. Three knocks and all is well. No knocks and all guns blazing. He dug in his jeans for the solitary key Redfern had given him.

Cochrane snatched the key out of Todd's grasp and stuck it in the lock.

Todd couldn't see around this one. It was a lose-lose situation. If he screamed out a warning to Redfern, his brains would be all over the wall before he got the first word out. If he stayed quiet, they'd have the drop on Redfern.

Then Todd saw the edge he needed. Cochrane and his linebackers weren't expecting anyone to be at home. Their artillery stayed firmly rested in holsters. Nobody had the drop on anyone. It was a fifty-fifty game. Not the greatest odds, but better than he was accustomed to sporting. Cochrane twisted the key and opened the door.

He went through the door first. The linebackers shoved Todd ahead of them.

"Collins, where the fuck have you been?" Redfern shouted from inside the apartment.

The four of them froze in the foyer to the apartment. This was a barrel shot for Redfern. The foyer was at the bottom of a long, narrow flight of stairs that led into the apartment. Redfern might be one gun against three, but his vantage point gave him the better odds.

Redfern's feet pounded on the hardwood floor. "What did I say about flying under the radar, dickhead?"

Cochrane fixed Todd with a look of pure hatred as he and his linebackers reached for their guns. Dalton released his hold on Todd and reached for his shoulder rig. Cochrane had his silenced pistol out. Redfern didn't stand a chance.

"We've got company," Todd shouted then dropped his shoulder and charged Cochrane. He slammed him into the wall and they both fell onto the stairs. The pistol bounced from Cochrane's grasp.

Redfern appeared at the top of the stairs with his gun drawn. He had a clear shot of the linebackers and they had a clear shot of him. Vasquez made the mistake of reaching for Todd to tear him off Cochrane. Redfern showed no mercy and drilled him with two rounds. The first caught Vasquez in the meat of his shoulder, but the second was a headshot that dropped him on the spot. He fell against the back of Todd's legs and Todd's grip on Cochrane slipped. Cochrane wriggled himself free from Todd and reached for his pistol.

Dalton got off a shot, but missed. Redfern ducked out of sight, then reappeared. He fired two rounds at the linebacker again. Redfern's bullets couldn't miss with that big a target and both rounds hit home in his chest. Dalton staggered back, hit the wall behind him and slid down. The linebacker got off three shots as he went down. One glanced off Redfern's head and he went down, falling out of sight.

Now it was just Todd and Cochrane. Todd shrugged Vasquez off his feet and lunged for the recovering small man. Cochrane swung his gun towards Todd. In the close quarters, Todd moved inside Cochrane's reach and batted his arm out of the way. Cochrane put too much effort into keeping a hold on his gun and Todd looped his handcuffed wrists over his neck. He jerked the short length of chain links into Cochrane's throat.

"Die, you bastard," Todd screamed.

"After you," Cochrane choked out. He reached his gun arm behind him to point the weapon straight at Todd's stomach.

Todd turned sideways to avoid the two shots. He twisted his wrists to tighten the garrote around Cochrane's throat and before

Cochrane could fire again, he threw his weight against Cochrane, driving him forward into the stairs. Cochrane's gun went off as his head bounced off the sharp edge of the stair. None of this deterred Cochrane. He bucked and jerked under Todd, fighting for any opportunity to get the better hand.

"Hold it right there."

Both of them froze.

Redfern stood at the top of the stairs with his gun pointed their way. Blood masked half his face where the bullet had creased the side of his head. He descended the top stair with the dexterity of a toddler's first steps and used the wall for support, but he never lost his aim.

"Is that you, Redfern?" Cochrane croaked. "I thought I'd crushed you a long time ago."

"Get him up, Todd."

Todd hoisted Cochrane to his feet with the handcuff noose as his helping hand. Cochrane choked out a gurgle.

"Drop the gun, Cochrane," Redfern ordered.

Cochrane hesitated.

"Do it."

Todd tightened his chokehold just to underline Redfern's request.

Cochrane dropped the gun. To Todd, it made the sweetest sound as it struck the stair.

"Where are the keys to the cuffs?" Redfern asked.

"My pocket," Cochrane said and indicated to his pants pocket.

Todd retrieved the keys and uncuffed himself.

Redfern took another unsteady step. "I'm going to enjoy saying this. You're under arrest."

"Boss," a voice from behind Todd murmured.

The voice weakened Todd's grasp.

Either reacting to the voice or Todd's weakening hold, Cochrane fired an elbow into Todd's gut. The blow connected with the bruises put there by Kenneth and Todd folded up. This unbalanced Cochrane and he pushed back on his heels to topple himself and Todd. Todd tried to stay upright, but he couldn't and he went down with Cochrane on top of him.

"Todd," Redfern shrieked, but the shots cut his cry short.

Dalton, with a clear target, hit Redfern twice in the chest. It was the last thing he did before he died.

Redfern's legs buckled and he crashed down on his back and slid down three stairs before he came to a halt.

Now on top of Todd, Cochrane jerked his head back and head-butted Todd in the face. Pain lit up like a flare in Todd's head when Cochrane connected with his nose. Blood poured immediately. Todd's cries spurred Cochrane on and he head-butted Todd twice more. Todd's grip around Cochrane's throat loosened and he threw Todd's arms over his head. He scrambled for his gun, grabbed it and swung it around at Todd. Todd lashed out with his only ready weapon, his feet. He smashed Cochrane in the chest, launching him backwards and tripping over the bottom stairs. Todd rolled backwards out the front door and fell down the marble steps. His bones impacted every sharp edge the hard stone had to offer. Cochrane fired twice. The bullets bit chunks out of the marble, the crack of the splitting stone louder than the silenced weapon.

Sirens wailed in the near distance.

Todd ran for his Toyota still parked where he left it. He expected bullets to punch holes in his back, but the bullets never came. Cochrane had his own problems to worry about. Todd reached his Toyota in time to see Cochrane racing over to the Lincoln.

Everyone had to cut and run sometime.

* * *

Traffic stopped Todd's escape from being a speedy one. He'd managed only half a dozen blocks before police units sped by him. None gave him a second look and he slowed. He didn't need to make his erratic driving memorable to all and sundry.

Without the fear of arrest occupying his thoughts, his predicament rushed in to fill the void. Redfern was dead. The last person who could help him out of this was dead. What did he do now? He could run back to Charlie Ruskin but why screw up her life just as it was on the level again? There was Fisk, but he'd made it very obvious that his return to the Emerald City wouldn't be appreciated. He had to face it; there wasn't a way out, not this time.

An additional weight pressed down on Todd. He had finally

done it. He'd gotten someone killed. And a cop at that. The SFPD had just turned into a lynch mob and they wouldn't care how many they had to string up to settle accounts.

The only thing going for him was that Cochrane was in the same position. Worse, even. It would take time before someone worked out Todd's identity from Redfern's files, but it wouldn't be necessary to look up Cochrane's info, not with the two linebackers dead on Redfern's doorstep. Cochrane would have to run now. He couldn't waste his time on settling a score with Todd, regardless of how large it had swelled with this latest development. Todd might not have to run if Cochrane ran first. The next few hours would determine everything. Todd could afford to weigh up his options. For now, he'd be okay if he kept circulating. He'd become a shark. As long as he kept moving, he'd stay alive.

The plan worked for a while. He threaded his way through the city's streets, shifting from one neighborhood to another. He listened to the radio for news. The stations reported a fatal shooting in Noe Valley, but released no details thanks to the police not providing any. That made sense. They didn't need the public's involvement. They knew the identities of all the players already.

Todd thought the cover of night would give him anonymity, but that went out of the window when he spotted a Dodge Magnum turning onto the street behind him. It could have been any Dodge Magnum, but he knew, just knew, it was the one belonging to Jeremiah Black's crew. Panic broke out in icy trails originating from the coldness in the pit of his stomach, but he kept his head. He could be wrong about the Dodge. It could be one of a hundred Magnums in the city. There was one way to find out.

He was on California. He took to his first right. The Dodge did likewise. His fingertips began to sweat and turned the wheel slick in his grasp. He made another right and another and another until he was back to where he started. Still the Dodge filled his rearview mirror.

So there it was. If the cops or Cochrane didn't get him, then Jeremiah Black would. Well, not if Todd could help it.

Todd stamped on the gas. The Toyota gathered speed. So did the Dodge.

He cut between cars and buses. Drivers honked at both him and the Dodge. He hoped one of the moving obstacles would do him a favor and collide with the Magnum, but none did.

The chase ended in Presidio Heights. Todd lunged across on-coming traffic to make an unexpected left. Black's crew didn't react in time and didn't make the turn. He expected them to appear a couple of blocks later, but they didn't. Had he done it? It looked that way after five minutes and he eased off the gas.

The Toyota's brakes felt spongy underfoot and he had to press harder than he should. He wanted to pull over, but the water temperature gauge was in the red so he drove around until the needle dropped back into the green. He pulled over and gave the Toyota a rest.

He'd no sooner switched the engine off when a blue Econoline van pulled up alongside him. Before the passenger finished winding down the van's window, Todd gunned the engine, but an Escalade pulled across the front to block his path and the Magnum stopped behind to box him in.

The person in the Econoline's passenger seat held Todd in place by poking a shotgun out of the open window. Todd raised his hands.

Four black guys poured from the Escalade and pulled him out of the car.

Kenneth emerged from the back of the Dodge Magnum.

"Don't think about yelling," he said. "It wouldn't help."

Todd glanced up at the townhouses with their lights on and drapes drawn. *So close yet so far*, he thought.

Kenneth ordered his guys to put Todd in the Dodge and told one of them to take care of Todd's Toyota. By the time Kenneth had slid next to Todd on the Dodge's backseat, the Econoline, the Escalade and Todd's Toyota were gone.

"Let's go,' Kenneth said to the driver.

"Where?" Todd asked.

"I'm going to let that be a surprise, white boy."

Kenneth struck with cobra's speed and tenacity. His hands snapped out, grabbed Todd and pulled him in close. He tied his arms in a knot around Todd's neck. Todd thrashed to stop Kenneth from breaking his neck. The other guy sandwiching Todd in the back seat smothered Todd's legs to prevent him from breaking loose.

"Don't fight it, Todd," Kenneth said.

But he had to fight. He didn't want to die. Not like this. It wasn't right and it wasn't fair. But when was anything fair? He clawed at the arm across the front of his throat. He wasn't going to let Kenneth break his neck.

But his neck didn't break. Instead, he slipped into darkness as consciousness let him fall.

* * *

A slap jerked Todd from the realms of unconsciousness. He found himself in the half-completed carcass of a building project. A couple of work lights lit the area. The framing and a little sheetrock was in place and made the large expanse of unoccupied space seem cramped. He sat with his legs splayed out in front of him with his back to one of the studs and his arms pinned behind him and cuffed around it. He was high up with a view of the Bay Bridge and the drone of the traffic rushing across it. He knew where he was. This was the Bay Towers, an exclusive SOMA condo development that came with a price tag that made most weep. *At last, I'm moving up in the world, just as I'm checking out of it*, he thought. He smiled at his own joke. He was too punchy to cry at it.

Cochrane had provided the slap. So Black had followed through on his promise and given him up for the points it would earn him. He tried to be angry, but couldn't. It was all way beyond petty squabbles now.

Cochrane looked a mess. He still wore the same ripped clothes as he'd worn earlier. Bruises had blossomed from their tussle on the stairs. Todd tried not to take pleasure from the purple necklace in the pattern of a handcuff chain across Cochrane's throat.

Cochrane jammed his pistol under Todd's chin. "I should fucking kill you and be done with it, but I can't let you off that easy."

Cochrane's cool was gone and along with it, his power of menace. Todd no longer found him frightening. He was nothing more than a barking dog staked to a spot in a backyard. True, the gun could end his life at the squeeze of a trigger, but that was inevitable and he couldn't be frightened of an inevitability. He wouldn't die in fear of Leo Cochrane and without that hanging over his head, things didn't seem so bad.

"I thought about turning you into a human torch. I even brought the gas along." He pointed at a plastic gas can behind him. "But I thought of something better." A sadistic leer spread across his face. "Where's my coke?"

"In a luggage locker at the Caltrain station on 4th Street."

"Where's the key?"

"In my pocket."

Cochrane rooted around in Todd's pockets. "You know what I'm going to do with the coke?"

Todd shook his head.

Cochrane jerked out the locker key. He held it up close to Todd's face like it was the Holy Grail. "I'm going to feed it to you. I'm going to watch you choke, spasm, convulse and die eating my coke."

"No, you're not."

The voice startled both Todd and Cochrane. Cochrane jerked his gun up in the direction of the voice.

"Put it down, Leo," the voice ordered. "It's over."

"Redfern," Todd said unconsciously.

Cochrane picked up on what Todd had said and the tension went out of his body. "Is that you, Redfern?"

Redfern emerged from the shadows with his gun aimed at Cochrane. A bandage replaced the blood Todd had last seen masking half his face.

"I thought you were dead."

"Kevlar, Leo. You've gotta love it."

"Wearing it now?"

"That would be telling."

"I can make a headshot."

Elation rushed Todd by surprise. It was over. Whatever Cochrane tried, it was over. SFPD and SWAT had it covered. Yet something was missing.

"Where's the backup, Redfern?" Todd asked.

Cochrane laughed. "What did he tell you? That's he's one of San Francisco's finest? Have you been fibbing to our friend here, Redfern?"

Redfern said nothing. He grimaced like he had the onset of a migraine and maintained his aim on Cochrane.

"Redfern, here, hasn't been a cop in five years."

How have I been so stupid? Todd thought. He'd never seen any ID, just the shield. And how hard was it to get one of those? He wanted to be sick.

"Rumors of taking bribes, wasn't it? Bribes paid by me to you, wasn't that it, Redfern?"

"You framed me."

"And you think this is going to win you back your career. Is that it? This isn't a movie. Hell, not even a TV movie."

"Just put the gun down and give yourself up. That's all I want."

"You make it sound so easy, but I'm sorry. No Hollywood endings this time around."

Todd saw Cochrane's trigger finger tighten. Cochrane was still crouched over him, still within reach. Todd snapped out a leg a second before Cochrane fired. His foot smashed into Cochrane's hip, knocking him on his side and sending the bullet wild.

Cochrane swung the gun around on Todd. Hatred burned up his features a moment before a bullet from Redfern's gun tore it away. The impact jerked his head around before he collapsed on his back.

Redfern rushed in and kicked the pistol from Cochrane's hand. He fired a glance Todd's way. "You okay?"

"As soon as the cops get here."

* * *

Hotel life was taking its toll on Todd, mainly around the waistline. Normality would resume in the coming days. The San Francisco Police Department's investigation was drawing to a close and ending his free stay at the Holiday Inn Fisherman's Wharf. When he wasn't giving statements, he was exploring the city, for once as a tourist. When he lived there, he never got to this stuff, but with the speed of a major criminal investigation, there was plenty of free time.

After returning from a tour of Alcatraz, he was walking back to his room when a midnight blue Bentley Continental GT pulled up next to him. The window glided down into the recesses of the passenger door and Jeremiah Black leaned over from the driver's side.

"Get in." When Todd didn't move, he said, "Look, you're cool. I'm alone. My boys aren't around. They're plenty busy, thanks to you. I just want to talk. Get in. Please."

Todd eyed the street for the Dodge Magnum or any other suspicious vehicles in the vicinity. He saw none and got into the car. Black pulled away and Todd watched his hotel get small in the distance.

Today, Black had left the sharp suit at home and had gone with an urban look. The contrast went well with the best-that-money-could-buy automobile.

"Nice ride," Todd said.

"Nice? Are you tripping? This is a premium ride."

"My mistake. What do you want?"

"You're a suspicious son of a bitch, aren't you? Can't a man say thank you?"

"Not when you served me up to Leo Cochrane."

"That? You're going to let something as small as that come between you and me?" He sucked air through his teeth and shook his head in mock disgust.

Todd decided he was trying a little too hard with all this. It was time to keep it real.

"You masterminded all this, didn't you?"

Black attempted a poker face, but the gleam in his eyes gave him away.

"I've had plenty of time to think all this through. Redfern, Cochrane, they didn't fall upon me just because I gave off some scent. They were pointed at me and you did the pointing."

"So you found me out."

Black steered the Bentley onto the Embarcadero and drove slow. The car caught every pedestrian's eye. Todd guessed half of them thought they'd caught a glimpse of some celebrity.

"I knew Leo and Redfern had clashed in the past at Redfern's expense. He's a private citizen and I had someone whisper in his ear that it might be worth his while to follow you because you might just lead him to Leo and a crock of drugs. I spiced it up with the idea he might win his job back—and he has, so I hear."

Pending an internal investigation, Redfern would wear his shield again, but not in his old capacity. What capacity it would be, only politics would decide. That had been Redfern's opinion when Todd had spoken to him last.

"I had to tell Leo so that he and Redfern could collide."

"You used me as bait."

"I object to that. Bait is expendable. You were never in any danger. My boys had your back. They would have swooped in if you'd needed saving." Black laughed. "I gotta say you shaved a few years off their lives with all the fireworks at Redfern's crib."

"With Leo out of the way, I just made you king."

He smiled. "And your monarch thanks you."

"I thought you weren't interested in rocking the boat. You were happy with your turf."

"Did you think I was going to tell you anything? Besides, I told you that I wasn't going to be your trigger man."

"Instead, I became yours."

"I think it's time you chilled out. I came here to say thanks."

"For what?"

"For being a good soldier."

Todd saw where this was going. "Hey, I don't work for you."

"But you can."

"No thanks."

"Can't work for a brother. Is that it?"

"No. I've been in the firing line one too many times of late and I'm looking for a different career. I don't need thanking. Leo Cochrane is off my back and everything is right with the world."

"Then what am I going to do with what's under your seat?"

Todd pulled out a nylon bag. The material was so flimsy it was easy to tell what it contained. He unzipped it for confirmation and came face to face with a brick of hundred dollar bills six inches thick.

"I shouldn't take this."

"Why?"

"Because you'll have something on me. It'll keep me quiet about your involvement."

"But you're going to take it."

Todd smiled. "Oh, yeah."

Black stopped the car in the shadow of SBC Park. "Just tell me you won't piss it away and you'll do something good with it."

"I will."

They shook hands and Todd got out of the car. Black roared away.

Todd glanced back up the Embarcadero. He had a long walk back to his hotel ahead of him. He could catch a cab. He could afford it, but he doubted that a taxi driver could break a couple of hundred thousand. He liked the idea of a walk.

He pulled out his cell phone and punched in Charlie Ruskin's number. They'd been in touch constantly since Redfern had killed Cochrane. A bond had grown between them and he liked that. She answered on the second ring.

"How'd it go today?" she asked.

He filled her in on the finer and duller details of the investigation. He didn't want to talk about it and switched subjects.

"How's business?" he asked.

"Fine. Inventory is turning over."

"What are your prospects?"

"Good. This is Texas. Everyone has to own at least one car. Why all the questions?"

Todd cast an eye down at his money in its nylon bag. "I was wondering if you'd be interested in taking on a partner."

"What makes you think you can sell cars?"

"You wouldn't believe the skills I have."